D0056982

HIDE AND SEEKER

HIDE AND SEEKER

DAKA HERMON

Scholastic Press / New York

Library of Congress Cataloging-in-Publication Data

Names: Hermon, Daka, author.
Title: Hide and seeker / Daka Hermon.
Description: First edition. | New York: Scholastic Press, 2020. | Audience: Grades 4–6. | Summary: Something is wrong with twelve-year-old Zee, who has returned after a year's absence; nobody knows where he was or what happened to him, but now he is distracted and violent, freaking out when he sees his friends, Justin, Nia, and Lyric, playing an odd game of hide-and-seek, and talking wildly about some danger that is approaching—and soon his friends are pulled into a shadowy world ruled by a monstrous, shape-shifting Seeker, forced to play a terrifying game of hide-and-seek where they will have to confront their worst nightmares in order to find their way home.
Identifiers: LCCN 2020000071 (print) | LCCN 2020000072 (ebook) | ISBN 9781338583625 (hardcover) | ISBN 9781338583649 (ebk)
Subjects: LCSH: Missing children—Juvenile fiction. | Hide-and-seek—Juvenile fiction. | Monsters—Juvenile fiction. | Fear—Juvenile fiction. | Friendship—Juvenile fiction. | Horror tales. | CYAC: Horror stories. | Missing children—Fiction. | Hide-and-seek—Fiction. | Monsters—Fiction. | Fear—Fiction. | Friendship—Fiction. | LCGFT: Horror fiction.
Classification: LCC PZ7.1.H492 Hi 2020 (print) | LCC PZ7.1.H492 (ebook) | DDC 813.6 [Fic]—dc23
LC record available at https://lccn.loc.gov/2020000071
LC ebook record available at https://lccn.loc.gov/2020000072

3 2020

Printed in the U.S.A. 23
First edition, September 2020

Book design by Stephanie Yang

FOR MY MOM AND DAD, MARY AND JOSEPH HERMON,

WHO ALWAYS BELIEVED.

FOR MY GRANDMA FLORENCE DELORIS VAUGHN,

WHO IS THE REASON I KNOW SUPERHEROES ARE REAL.

01

Zee never shoulda come back. Not like this.

Limp blue balloons and crinkled streamers are tangled around the mailbox at the end of Zee's driveway. I adjust my sweaty baseball cap and sigh. Not even the decorations are excited about his welcome home party.

A fat gray cloud settles directly above the house. Shadows play across the tattered roof shingles, and trails of dirt, like black tears, streak the windows. I shiver as beads of sweat roll down the sides of my hot face.

"Justin," a voice screeches.

I spin around. My friend Nia skips down the sidewalk carrying a small wrapped box.

"Hey." She skids to a halt. Her long braids flap out behind her like a superhero cape in the wind. She extends her fist and smiles so big her dimples bite into her chipmunk cheeks.

"Hey." I bump her knuckles with mine. I haven't seen her since we met up for the Fourth of July fireworks last week. They're legal in Chattanooga, so the sky was lit up most of the night.

"I love that shirt," she says.

I study my wrinkled *Star Wars* T-shirt. Most of the design has faded. Only the outline of Darth Vader's helmet and the words "I am" remain.

"Let me fill in the blank. I am . . . happy to see you," she says with a giggle.

I roll my eyes and point to the box she's holding. "What's that?"

"A welcome home present for Zee. New paintbrushes." She bites the corner of her lower lip. "It's from both of us. I figured you'd be thinking about other things."

Yeah, my "other things" list is so long I trip over it when I walk. I shift from foot to foot. "Uh, thanks."

She stares at something over my shoulder. "That's the second one I've seen since I left my house."

I turn. A police car cruises down the street. There's been a lot more patrols lately.

"C'mon." She tugs me up the driveway.

I drag my feet. "We're early. Maybe—"

"Four hundred and four days," says Nia.

"What?"

"Zee disappeared four hundred and four days ago. It's been one year, one month, and nine days since we've seen him. That's a *long* time."

It's still fresh. I didn't think things could get any worse after Zee went missing, but seven days after that I was proven wrong.

I trip over my feet as Nia pulls me up the creaking porch steps. The front door flies open. Mrs. Murphy, Zee's mom, stands in the doorway smiling like she won the Tennessee Mega Lottery. She didn't.

"Y'all came. I wasn't sure . . . Zechariah is gonna be so happy," says Mrs. Murphy.

Zee's real name is Zechariah Murphy; his mom named him after some prophet in the Bible. We call him Zee 'cause it's easier and sounds cooler—no offense to the Bible guy.

"How are you, sweetie? Your family okay?" The questions sprint out of Mrs. Murphy's mouth like they're in a fifty-yard dash.

Nia nods. "Yep. We're all good. We just got back from our family reunion."

"Was it fun?" Mrs. Murphy asks, running her hand over Nia's long braids.

"Yeah, I got to see my grandma," Nia says with a heavy sigh. "She didn't remember me at first. My mom told me forgetting stuff can happen when you get old."

"That's true," says Mrs. Murphy.

"Well, I don't like it," says Nia. "I wish people didn't have to grow old. My grandma can't even move around that much, but we still had some fun. We played our favorite game, Did You Know?"

"I'm glad you were able to spend some time with her," says Mrs. Murphy.

"Yeah," Nia says quietly, then she smiles. It's not as bright as usual. "Did you know about ninety-six percent of families create cool T-shirts for their family reunions?"

Mrs. Murphy shakes her head. "I didn't know that." Her dark hair swings back and forth, revealing chunks of new gray strands. "Did your family make shirts?"

Nia snorts. "Nope. We're part of the lame four percent." She holds up the present. "We brought Zee something. It's not a T-shirt."

"You didn't have to do that, but I'm sure he'll love whatever it is." Mrs. Murphy pats Nia's cheek. "And thank you for the care package. It meant a lot."

Care package? Great. I feel lower than gum on the bottom of a shoe. Since Zee was released from the hospital two weeks ago, I've only stopped by once, to tie a "Welcome Home" balloon on the mailbox. I didn't even go inside to see him. "WORST FRIEND EVER" should be tattooed on my forehead in all caps. It's just . . . I didn't want to see him so messed up. Still don't.

Mrs. Murphy turns to me. "Hi, baby." She tugs me close.

Air swooshes out of my lungs. A mom hug.

One week after Zee disappeared, my mom died. That means it's been 397 days since I've heard her voice, seen her smile, felt her arms around me.

I sink into Mrs. Murphy's round, soft body. She smells like flowers and chocolate. For a moment I can pretend she's mine, then a tidal wave of sadness crashes over me.

Three hundred and ninety-seven days. I know Nia didn't mean to do it, but now I have a count stuck in my head. I've heard people say that losing someone doesn't hurt as much after a while. They're wrong. The pain is still there, but it's not constant. I have sneak attacks. You feel okay for an hour or a day, then BAM! You experience the heartbreak all over.

I wiggle free of Mrs. Murphy.

Her piercing gaze roams over my face. I pretend not to notice the puffiness under her tired eyes. "How ya doing?" she asks.

I slide my hat back over my short locs. "I'm good."

With a weak smile, she straightens her loose dress. "I wanted to thank you again for taking out my trash and cutting the grass while Zechariah was, uh, gone all that time. You were dealing with—"

"I had to mow other lawns anyway, and I didn't mind helping out," I say. "Zee would have done the same for me."

Mrs. Murphy squeezes my shoulder. "I'm sorry I wasn't able to be there for you when your mom—"

"It's fine." My chest tightens. I stuff my trembling hand into the right back pocket of my jeans and clutch a knobby puzzle piece. After several deep breathes the pain in my chest eases.

"I . . . I told Zee about your mom," she says softly.

I bite the inside of my cheek. "How did he . . . Was he okay?" Another person he loved was gone. Zee's dad died in a car accident when he was four.

Mrs. Murphy blinks hard, and I hope she doesn't start crying. I couldn't handle that. "It's been hard for him. Everything's hard right now."

I nod. He would have wanted to say goodbye, be there for her funeral. That's another reason why his disappearance was so strange. He'd never miss it on purpose.

"When Zee was gone I always had this feeling he was close, but I . . ." She swallows hard.

"Yeah." I get it. Sometimes it was like Zee was right beside me. Like I sensed his presence, but I think it was because I missed him so much.

"You never gave up," she says. "You said he'd come back and you were right." Mrs. Murphy gestures for us to enter.

I step inside the house. My feet hit shattered picture frames propped up near the doorway. A dirty sheet covers the hardwood floor, and two paint cans sit by the couch. Leaning against a chair, there's a large canvas forest painting with a slash mark down the middle.

My eyes travel over the walls. Dark smudges and deep scratches are visible underneath the new layer of white paint. I shudder as a chill tiptoes up and down my spine.

"Sorry about the mess. I haven't had time to straighten up," Mrs. Murphy says. "I've been busy."

Mrs. Murphy has always kept a clean house. This isn't like needing to dust or vacuum. The living room isn't dirty. It's damaged.

"You, uh, redecorating?" Nia glances around.

"Zee . . . He's adjusting to being home again," Mrs. Murphy says as she smooths out invisible wrinkles in her dress.

There are scratches all down her arms. She catches me staring and slides her hands in her pockets.

I lower my gaze. What happened to her? Would Zee . . . No. He'd never hurt his mom. Not on purpose.

Nia side-eyes me. "Is everything okay, Mrs. Murphy?"

"Yes, of course. I—"

A loud buzzer sound causes us all to jump.

"That's just the stove. The cake is ready," says Mrs. Murphy.

I dry my sweaty hands on my jeans. My heart is racing and I'm not sure why.

"I knew I smelled sweetness." Nia smiles, but it's too bright. Not real.

"Chocolate Coca-Cola cake," Mrs. Murphy says, closing the front door behind us.

"Soda *in* a cake? That's brilliant," says Nia. "And I'm madly in love with chocolate. It's my favorite food group. Top of the pyramid."

"I'll make sure you get an extra big piece to take home. And, Justin, I'll pack up a slice for Victoria," says Mrs. Murphy.

"Thanks." My sister loves Coca-Cola cake. My mom used to make it all the time.

"Why don't y'all head out back?" Mrs. Murphy directs us toward the kitchen back door.

I hesitate, glancing over my shoulder at the mess in the living room. "Are you sure everything is alright?"

Her eyes shift quickly from me as she chews on her bottom lip. "This party will be good for Zee. He needs to be around his friends. He's a little nervous to see everyone."

Nia and I exchange a startled look. Is Mrs. Murphy saying Zee made this mess? What is going on?

"It's fine. I promise," Mrs. Murphy says with extra cheer. "Everyone will have a great time."

She stares, her eyes pleading for us to agree. I have so many questions rattling around in my head, but I don't feel like I can ask them.

"We can't wait to see Zee. We'll have fun," Nia says.

I nod, but I'm worried. Something is not right.

"Lyric's already here." Mrs. Murphy urges us toward the back door. "He wants to provide the musical entertainment."

Nia groans. I laugh weakly. This could be interesting.

"He brought his harmonica, didn't he?" Nia asks.

Mrs. Murphy nods, her expression pained. "I got a preview. He *is* better."

Lyric loves music. And he plays lots of instruments, just not well. But I give him big props for his dedication.

"The tables are all set up. I'll bring some more snacks out in a little while," says Mrs. Murphy as Nia walks out the back door.

I glance down the hall toward Zee's bedroom. Three gold dead bolts on the outside of his door catch my eye. My gaze darts toward Mrs. Murphy. "What . . . ?"

She twists her hands. "Zee's not himself yet. He still has some rough nights. Nightmares and sleepwalking . . . I don't want him getting out and hurting himself."

I gulp. Zee isn't getting better. Nobody knows why he disappeared over a year ago and how he turned up miles from home, wandering in the woods and covered in scars. Zee can't explain what happened.

"He'll be okay," I say because she needs encouragement. So do I.

Mrs. Murphy blinks back tears and smiles.

"Justin!" Nia yells.

With one last look down the hall at the door dead-bolted shut, I hurry outside to see Lyric hunched over a table shoveling food into his mouth. His mountain of wild curls casts a large shadow across the bowls of snacks. Though we're all heading into sixth grade, he's almost a foot taller because of his super-sized blond hair.

He smiles. Popcorn kernels are wedged between the gaps in his teeth. "Sup, y'all? Way to roll up all late and stuff."

"The party invite said Friday at four p.m." Nia removes her phone from her back pocket and glances at the screen. "It's 4:07."

"I was here at 3:45," Lyric says.

Nia sticks out her tongue. "Whatev. You came early for the food."

"True, true."

I glance around. No Zee.

"Hey, man!" Lyric says, jolting me out of my troubled thoughts.

He extends his fist. I bump it with mine. Lyric is the only white kid in our neighborhood. His family moved here right before we started first grade and we've been tight ever since.

The Fantastic Four. That's what we called ourselves—me, Nia, Lyric, and Zee. We were together so much our families joked that we shared the same brain. Well, until my mom got sick and Zee disappeared.

Nia sets our present down on the table next to a small object wrapped with newspaper and duct tape.

"What's that?" I point to Lyric's gift.

"An awesomely great surprise for Zee." Lyric chomps on some candy. "No peeking," he says when Nia tries to inspect the package.

"It's a harmonica," she says with a confident smile.

Lyric throws up his hands. "How do you know that?"

"You called me after you found it at that thrift store. You went on and on about how music makes everything better, how your harmonica, the one you carry around with you everywhere, is the best gift you ever received and how one day when you're a famous musician you're gonna—"

"Okay, okay, Ruiner of Welcome-Home Surprises," Lyric grumbles. "Sometimes I hate that you remember everything."

Nia taps her head with her finger. "One day all the information stored in here could save your life. Knowledge is power, young one."

Lyric laughs. "Whatever. I just hope Zee likes my present. Maybe I'll teach him a song today if he's up to it."

Nia and I grimace.

Lyric removes his harmonica from the front pocket of his worn jeans and kisses it. "You're awesome," he says to the instrument.

"Have you seen Zee?" I ask.

Lyric shakes his head. "Not yet. And I stopped by a couple of days ago, but his mom said he wasn't feeling too good."

"Do you think this party's a good idea?" The locks on his door say maybe not.

Nia tucks some braids behind her ears. "I bet once he sees us he'll be fine. We can make him forget about whatever happened."

Lyric and I share a worried look. I hope she's right. We were hoping he might be able to start school with us once summer break is over. Now, I'm not so sure.

"Anybody want ice cream?" Lyric opens the top latch of a small, portable cart placed near the food table. "Sweet Dreams Homemade

Ice Cream—It'll make you scream!" is scrawled on the side of the cart in purple lettering. Underneath are peeling stickers displaying different types of treats—Popsicles, snow cones, Push-Up Pops, Drumsticks, sundae cups.

"How many have you had already?" I ask.

Lyric's lips twist to the side. "Two or three, maybe four."

Nia rolls her eyes and grabs a sundae cone cup. "You want one?" she asks me.

"Sure." She hands me a small ice cream cone. I sneak another peek at Zee's house as I remove the wrapper.

Inside, a door slams and muffled voices float out an open window. A shadow drifts across the backyard. I peer up at a black crow circling above. Two more join in the bird merry-go-round. They dive low to land on Zee's roof. Their heads twitch from side to side, then their marbled eyes lock on to me.

Caw, caw! a bird cries.

I jump. The ice cream slips out of my hand.

"Bad luck."

My gaze jerks to Nia. "What?"

"It's bad luck if you drop your ice cream and the cone hits the ground first," she says.

The cone is crushed and melting ice cream pools around it.

Lyric laughs. "You made that up."

"No, I didn't. I heard it somewhere. It's totally true."

I try to shake off the uneasy vibe twisting my gut. My gaze

travels around the backyard. The urge to leave is so strong I have to lock my knees to keep from moving.

"Oooooh, this is cool!" Nia holds up a wrapper. "Sweet Dreams has facts on their wrappers. Listen to this . . . Hide and Seek may have originated from a Greek game called"—she peers at the small paper—"apo-did-ras-kin-da."

"Say what, now?" Lyric asks.

"Apodidraskinda. I'll have to remember that," she says.

She memorizes random information. It's her thing. She likes knowing stuff and learning, but she's allergic to school. Nia says the lessons are boring and don't focus on the subjects she's interested in—everything not taught in our classes. She goes blank during tests, forgets all the information. Her grades don't reflect how smart she is.

Only a strict study schedule and academic plan designed by her parents saved her from repeating fifth grade. They're high school teachers with "unrealistic expectations"—Nia's words, not mine.

"What did your wrapper say?" Nia asks me.

With a sigh, I kneel down and peel the wrapper off the melting chocolate. "There is a Hide and Seek world championship held annually in Italy every summer. One year there were seventy teams." I toss the sticky paper in the trash and lick the chocolate off my fingers.

"Interesting," Lyric says. "Sweet Dreams is out here dropping knowledge with their sugary goodness. Listen to this . . ." He studies his Popsicle wrapper. "Hide and Seek is the most popular kid's party game."

"Really?" Nia's face scrunches into a frown. "That can't be right."

Lyric chews on his treat. His tongue and lips are blue. "Maybe we could play when—"

Suddenly, the backyard fence door swings open and smacks the small table with Zee's gifts. Lyric drops his treat and dives for the presents but misses. Aww, man, I hope nothing's broken.

"What up, losers?" a beastly voice asks. "Startin' the party without us?"

I groan. Forget a dropped ice cream cone. This is the real bad luck.

02

Carla Jenkins and her twin brother, Quincy, stroll into the backyard. My mom used to say they weren't bad kids, only misunderstood. Most days they're *really* misunderstood, especially Carla.

"Hey, Dumbo," she says to me.

I roll my eyes. I have big ears. It used to bother me, then Nia said that in some cultures big ears mean good luck and that you're a good listener. I'm not so sure about the luck part. When my mom was having really bad days, I would wiggle my ears and she would laugh like it was the best thing ever. For a little while she was happy, but then—I slam the door closed on those thoughts. I can't go there. It hurts too much.

Carla swats a sagging streamer as she walks around. "Is this it?"

She's in our grade, but people always think she's older. She's taller than all the other students at our school. Sometimes she has trouble sitting in the desks.

"Some welcome home party. This sucks," she says.

"It does now that you're here," Lyric mutters. He places the presents back on the table and moves so there is more space between him and Carla.

Her head snaps around, and she glares at Lyric. "Seen your daddy lately or you gotta wait until visiting hours?"

Lyric stiffens like concrete is flowing through his veins. Overall he's pretty chill about everything, but he has one button you don't push—the "don't talk about my family" button. Carla just stomped on it.

Red blotches appear on his neck and spread to his pale face. He steps to Carla. "What'd you say?"

Carla sticks her chin out. "You heard me."

This girl is acting all kinds of stupid. Lyric opens his mouth to say something, but Nia jumps between them and shoves Lyric back.

His right eye twitches and he never looks away from Carla, who smirks, flashing a crooked smile. Her mission to irritate is accomplished.

"Lyric, did you know that the most common types of bullying are verbal and social?" asks Nia. "She's all talk. Don't let her get to you."

"Whatever. He wasn't gon' do nothing," Carla says, popping a piece of candy into her big mouth.

"That wasn't nice," her younger brother, Quincy, says with a frown. He's smaller than Carla, and not as annoying most days.

She stares at him for a moment, then turns away to look for more treats.

Why did Mrs. Murphy have to invite them? I reach for the puzzle piece in my pocket. I run my fingers along the edge of the frayed cardboard.

After my mom died, I had to see a counselor because I had trouble dealing with everything going on. I missed her, missed Zee, and I felt too much at once. I hated the sessions at first because they didn't help, but after a few months I learned how to handle stuff. I haven't had a real bad panic attack in a month. I'm not gonna let them ruin my new record.

The back door squeaks open. Mrs. Murphy exits carrying a tray of bottled water and soda.

"Carla. Quincy. I didn't know you were here." She sets the drinks on a table.

"Yes, ma'am. We came in the back way." Carla smiles so sweet, I get a toothache.

Nia rolls her eyes. Lyric coughs and whisper-shouts, "Posers." He's lounging in a chair, with his long legs outstretched. He looks relaxed, but I know better. The anger is still simmering in his blue eyes.

"I'm glad you made it." Mrs. Murphy peeks over her shoulder. "Zee is almost ready."

I exchange a glance with Nia. What's taking so long?

Lyric pushes to his feet and walks toward the house. "I can help—"

"No!" says Mrs. Murphy.

We jump.

She laughs nervously. "Everything is under control. I just want all of you to have fun."

"How?" Carla asks, with her hands on her hips.

"Why don't y'all play a game until I send Zee out?" Mrs. Murphy says, her eyes pleading with me. "I'm sure you can come up with something."

I hold back a sigh. "Yeah, we can figure it out."

"Thank you," Mrs. Murphy says.

There is a loud crash from inside the house.

"I'll be right back." She hurries up the stairs and through the back door.

Nia turns to me. "Justin—"

"What are we gonna play?" Quincy asks as he dances away from a large flying bug. His skinny arms rotate faster than blades on a fan. He swats the bug down to the ground and stomps on it until it's deader than dead. "Hate bugs," he mumbles.

"I wanna play Dodgeball," blurts out Carla.

Of course she does. The goal of the game is to hit someone.

Hard. She was captain of our school dodgeball team until she got kicked off for being too violent.

"No ball," Nia says.

"I knew that, stupid," Carla mutters.

Nia's eyes narrow. She crosses her arms. "Any fool can know. The point is to understand. Albert Einstein said that."

Carla stares blankly. "What?"

"Exactly." Nia holds up her closed fists and then opens her hand. She drops the mic. "Boom."

I rub a hand over my mouth to hide my smile. She's awesome.

"You're still stupid," Carla mumbles. "Remembering all that weird stuff doesn't make you smarter or better than me."

"What about Freeze Tag?" asks Quincy.

"No." Lyric shoves a hand through his wild hair. "Red Light, Green Light?"

"How about Hide and Seek?" a whiny voice suggests.

We all spin around. *Shae Davidson*? Mrs. Murphy must have been desperate when she created this guest list. Sure, we all live in the same neighborhood, but we aren't *friends*—she's not welcome-home-party worthy for sure. Shae, Carla, and Quincy don't belong. When you force things that don't fit together, it ruins everything.

Shae's lips twitch to form a smirk. "Hi, everybody."

"Why am I being punished?" Lyric mumbles with a groan.

Shae's family has money. They're not rich or anything, but they have the nicest house and cars on our block, and their grass is always green and cut low. They act like they're better than the rest of the neighbors.

"What are *you* doing here?" Carla asks, crossing her arms.

"I'm here for the party." Shae brushes past Quincy as she enters the backyard.

"Hi, Shae." He watches her, his eyes full of beating hearts. "You look sparkly. I like your . . . oomph."

Carla elbows him in the side. "Don't talk to her."

Doubled over, Quincy mumbles, "Sorry."

Shae toys with the long brown braid coiled on top of her head. "Hide and Seek is the best and we have enough people to play."

Nia side-eyes me. Shae never plays with us. She doesn't like to get dirty, sweaty, or smelly—her words. Sometimes she watches us, but always from a distance, usually where there's shade.

"There's not many places to hide," says Lyric. "What if—"

"Sounds good to me," Carla says, cracking her knuckles.

"Say what?" I jerk my head toward her so fast I almost get whiplash. Not more than a second ago she was shutting Shae down. "Why?"

Carla shrugs. "Not many choices since we don't have a ball."

"Justin?" Nia says, her expression pained.

Indigestion and nausea play tag in my stomach. "Fine, whatever." Anything to get this over with.

"Who wants to be the Seeker?" Lyric asks.

No one volunteers.

"I'll do it," I say with a heavy sigh. Shouldn't be too hard. It's gonna be a foot race and I'm fast.

Shae stands up straighter. Her attention is focused on me. I'm a bug under a microscope. "Rules?"

"Duuuuh," says Carla with an eye roll. "Same as always."

"If I tag you, you're out," I say. "You can't reveal the hiding place of another player. Can't hide inside a building or car. Only hide in the set backyard area. You can't block home base from any player. No roughing up anybody. Touch home base to be safe. And we have to finish the game. There has to be a clear winner." I've witnessed too many arguments and fights over games that were suspended because of darkness or pee breaks.

We form a circle. I extend my arm. Lyric places his hand over mine, then Nia adds hers. Quincy and Carla are next. Finally, Shae's hand slowly falls on top of the pile. A static shock zips up my arm.

My eyes dart around the group. They all have strange looks on their faces, like they felt something, too. Well, everyone except Shae, who stares at Zee's house with an odd smile.

"The rules are set. If you break them, you're out," I say, mostly to Shae since she doesn't seem to be paying attention. I don't wanna hear any whining later about being confused.

I wait for everyone to accept the rules, then lower my hand from the pile and flex my tingling fingers. I nod toward the large oak tree in the center of the backyard. "That'll be home base."

"Got it." Shae blinks rapidly and for a moment her eyes are the color of midnight, then they shift back to their normal green.

I step back. An eerie sensation weaves its way through me.

"What's wrong?" Nia says.

"Uh, nothing. Just the sunlight . . . I'm seeing things."

"Let's do this, losers." Carla shoulder checks me as she strolls by.

My mom used to say I shouldn't hate "nouns"—a person, a place, or a thing. Carla is a person; does that mean I can't hate her? Because most days I do.

I give everyone a moment to strategize as I walk over to the lonely oak tree standing between the sagging back porch and the snack tables. Its limbs droop from heat exhaustion. I slide my hat around so the brim is facing the back, close my eyes, and rest my head on folded arms. The rough bark makes small imprints in my skin. A bee buzzes around my head and the sound matches the odd static that fills my ears. I mentally shake myself and focus on the game.

"I went up the hill, the hill was muddy, stomped my toe and made it bloody, should I wash it?" I yell.

"Yes," the players shout from different locations as they search for hiding places.

The hot wind pants through the trees, and dead leaves shower down upon me.

"I went up the hill, the hill was muddy, stomped my toe and made it bloody, should I wash it?"

"Yes!" I recognize Carla's and Lyric's voices. They're still looking for a hiding spot.

"I went up the hill, the hill was muddy, stomped my toe and made it bloody, should I wash it?"

The backyard is eerily silent; it's holding its breath. No responses. They're ready.

I lift my head and slowly turn around. Brown brittle grass and wild weeds peekaboo out of the thirsty ground. Candy and ice cream wrappers chase each other like tumbleweeds.

The hunt begins.

I creep away from home base, my eyes skating across the backyard. Movement near the porch catches my attention. Carla. Somehow, she's managed to squeeze herself into the small crawl space.

A twig snaps under my foot as I prowl closer to tag her. The tablecloth flutters around the snack table. Nia rolls from underneath and races toward home base. I bolt forward, and then skid to a halt. No chance.

She smacks the tree and performs a few cheerleader high kicks. "Safe. I'm first. So cool. I rule."

With an eye roll, I walk toward Carla. Wedged in so tight, she'll be an easy out for sure.

"Shae's hiding behind the house!" she yells.

"Hey, no fair!" Nia cries.

"You can't—" I stumble back as Shae slinks from behind the side of the house. She watches me with an unblinking stare. Her lips curl back over her teeth in a creepy smile. My skin crawls.

"What, uh, are you still playing?" I ask. "You have to touch the tree to be safe, remember?"

She doesn't respond and makes no move toward home base.

Caw. Caw. The crows burst from the treetops, blasting leaves into the air. I jump.

"Shae, what—"

Suddenly, the shed door flies open, slamming against the wall. Quincy rushes out. His eyes widen when he spots me so close. He recovers and scrambles for the tree.

"Get him, Justin," Nia cries.

"Don't you touch my brother." Carla scoots from underneath the porch on her stomach. She crawls to her feet covered in dirt and cobwebs. "I'll hurt you."

With a growl, Lyric pops up from his hiding spot. "You better not touch him," he says to Carla.

My head whips back and forth. Shae. Carla. Quincy. Lyric. What is happening? It's chaos.

"Both of you are cheaters!" Lyric races toward Quincy.

Nia blocks Quincy's path, with her arms extended so he can't get close to the tree.

Lyric grabs his shirt and tugs him back. There's a struggle and they hit the ground, arms and legs tangled.

With a loud growl, Carla charges toward me. My eyes widen.

She lifts her fist and my short life flashes before my eyes. There's no dramatic music to match the action; instead I hear the happy jingle of an ice cream truck in the distance. Suddenly, she skids to a stop. Her jaw drops.

I spin around. Zee stands on his back porch. His glasses are heavily taped at the corners and slightly tilted on his thin face.

"His arms," Nia says shakily.

Lines of jagged, puffy scratches are on both of Zee's arms. The scars are shiny. A beam of sunlight hits them, and they appear to glow. I gulp.

Lyric jumps up and inhales a loud breath. "What . . ."

He steps forward. We all fall back.

"Hi, Zee." Shae waves. "Miss me?"

"No! You can't be here! How are you here?" he shouts.

My eyes shift back and forth between Shae and Zee. What is going on?! Zee and Shae aren't real friends, but he'd never be this rude to her. He'd never kick her out of his party.

"I came to get what's mine. You wouldn't play, but your friends did," says Shae. "Now I get everything I wanted. Isn't this fun?"

Zee shakes so hard, I swear I hear his bones rattle. His eyes dart around our group before zeroing in on me. "What did you do? I didn't want this! You should have stayed away!"

My heart skips. "Zee . . ."

"Out of the darkness, no more light, now it comes to steal your life. On this day you've sealed your fate, by playing what it loves to hate. Once you're tagged, then you'll know. The mark appears, it's your time to go," Zee chants. "Now you're in the final count. It's closer to the set amount."

"Whoa," Lyric says.

Quincy shuffles back a few steps. "What's wrong with him?"

"He ain't right," says Carla. "He came back wrong."

Zee's dazed eyes bob for apples. Up, down. Up, down. Now the locks on his bedroom door make sense.

Shae giggles, only it comes out like a growl. "This is so much fun."

"Hey!" I say. "Stop messin' with him. He's—"

"I won't let you do this! Leave us alone!" He leaps off the porch and dashes toward us.

Someone screams. We scatter like cockroaches in the light.

03

Zee staggers forward. "You can't let it win. You have to stop it!"

"I'm outta here!" Carla races past Nia, spinning her around and into a bush.

"Wait for me," Quincy cries as he trips over his feet to catch up with his sister. They escape through the fence door.

Wide-eyed, Lyric backpedals as Zee dashes in his direction. "Whoa! Hold up. What's going on?" Arms flailing, Lyric crashes into a table, sending the snacks flying across the backyard.

Shae is a pink blur. I used to run track, but I've never seen anyone move like that. She disappears around the side of the house.

I'm too stunned to move and that costs me. Zee swerves in my direction and tackles me. My head hits the ground with such force, black dots swim across my eyes and my hat sails across the lawn. I groan as he flips me over like a pancake. His body is a mini iceberg on my chest. I'm chilled to the bone.

"Hi, Justin," he whispers. The words are so eerily soft the breeze carries them away as soon as they leave his chapped lips.

I stare into his haunted eyes. "Hi . . . hi, Zee."

His mouth twists upward in the saddest smile I've ever seen. He leans closer and the smell of mothballs and baby powder tickle my nose.

"Because of me, it came."

"It? What are you talking about?" I strain away from him, pressing myself into the bumpy ground. Jagged rocks and sharp twigs dig into my back.

His head jerks up and his wild eyes travel around the backyard. His body is still, tense. "Watching," he whispers.

I get goose bumps.

Nia crawls closer. "Zee? What—"

He snaps out of his trance. "From the dark side it came to see, I failed the test it gave to me. It never loses; the rules aren't fair. And now you have to live the scare." His bony fingers handcuff my wrists. "One day soon you'll leave from here and fight against all you fear."

His words tornado through me. I feel a panic attack clawing at my skull. I struggle to get free, but he won't budge. "Get off me! Move."

"It's stronger now, it has more power." He grabs my shoulders and shakes me until the backyard and sky are a messy splash of colors. "You should have stayed away. I didn't want you to come. I tried to tell her. Why didn't she listen? I still lost. Now you're lost, too."

Suddenly Zee is gone and I can breathe again. I look over and see Lyric wrestling him to the ground. Zee flops and thrashes around like a fish on dry land.

"Don't touch me! Don't touch me!" Zee yells.

Wide-eyed, I stare at him, trembling all over. He tackled me, now *he* doesn't want to be touched?

"You okay?" Nia helps me sit up.

"No." How can I be? Zee attacked me.

"Justin. Please. Promise you'll stop it," Zee pleads, his voice suddenly normal, not as creepy.

I flinch. Promises. I *hate* promises. They're stupid. Just future lies wrapped with a big bow of disappointment. Everybody knows that.

"I went up the hill, the hill was muddy, stomped my toe and made it bloody, should I wash it?" Zee robotically chants. He tries to pull free of Lyric.

"Stop it, man. I don't wanna hurt you." Lyric sits on Zee's legs and pins down his arms.

Nia squeezes my hand. "Wh-what happened to him? Why is he acting like this?"

The back door squeaks open and Mrs. Murphy steps outside. "Okay, everybody. Cake time. Come and—"

She gasps when she spots us sprawled on the ground. The chocolate cake falls from her hands and goes splat on the porch.

"Zechariah? Oh no." She stumbles down the steps, slips on the icing and awkwardly lands near Zee on the ground. She tugs him into her arms, rocking him like a baby. He flinches. "Oh, sweetie. What happened?"

"He totally flipped out." The words burst out of me all alien-like.

Mrs. Murphy cradles his dirty face in her trembling hands. "Honey, are you okay?"

"Mom?" he moans and buries his head in her chest.

I swallow hard and glance away. The moment hurts.

"The party was a mistake. It was too soon. I'm sorry." Mrs. Murphy crumbles. The faucet turns on and the trickle of tears becomes a river flooding down her face. "He got so upset when I told him about the party, so angry . . ." Her voice cracks.

"Did he make that mess in the living room? Break the glass, scratch up the walls?" Nia asks.

Mrs. Murphy nods.

I exhale a shaky breath. Zee said he's lost. Does that mean he can't control himself? Maybe he should see my counselor. There has to be some way to help him.

"I just wanted things to go back to normal," Mrs. Murphy says.

"I was hoping if he spent time with his friends, he'd get better faster. That my Zee would come back." She sniffs. "Are you all okay?"

My cut lip stings. My arms ache from Zee's grip. You can probably play connect the dots with the bruises on my back, but I can't hurt Mrs. Murphy. "I'm fine."

"It's all good," Lyric says, though he doesn't look so confident. "No worries."

"Yeah." Nia smiles weakly. "Things just got a little physical . . . and I almost peed my pants." She whispers the last part.

"What happened to him?" I ask. "The scars . . ."

Mrs. Murphy's face scrunches as if she's in pain. "I don't know. When they found him, he—"

Zee lets out a loud moan and squirms out of his mom's embrace as if he's attempting to escape.

"I should take him inside. He should lie down," Mrs. Murphy says. "Shhhhh, baby. It's okay. I'm here."

He calms enough for her to get him on his feet. He sways a little. I reach out to steady him, but he jerks away.

His tortured eyes lift until he meets my gaze. "I'm sorry," he says.

There's a lot of things he could be apologizing for—hurting his mom, breaking stuff, all the shouting and screaming, chasing his party guests, attacking me—but I have a feeling that isn't what he's talking about.

"Why're you sorry?" I search his eyes, hoping to see my friend.

Tears trail down his dirty cheeks. "Ticktock. Ticktock. Bye-bye, Justin."

I flinch away from him. "What . . . what does that mean?"

"He's just confused," Mrs. Murphy says. "Let's go lie down, Zechariah."

"One, two, three, four. It came and wants to settle the score. Five, six, seven, eight. Darkness and terror are now your fate. Four hundred is the special number, to release it from its world of slumber," Zee shouts as his mom tugs him inside the house. The door slams shut.

Lyric inhales loudly. "What the—?"

I'm cold. Now hot. Cold again. I clench my clammy hands into fists and inhale several deep breaths.

"Why was he counting? Settle what score?" Nia asks with wild eyes. "Fate? World of what?"

Lyric pushes his hair off his wide forehead. "I'm kinda freaked out right now. That was messed up. Man, what happened to him while he was gone? I get he's, like, traumatized and stuff, but the old Zee would never have come at us like that."

Lyric continues to ramble, but his voice is a buzz of nonsense. The muscles tighten in my chest so it's hard to breathe. Inhale. Exhale. I reach for my puzzle piece.

What if Zee's stuck like this?

I grab my hat off the ground and race out of the backyard.

"Hey," Lyric says. "Wait!"

I speed up, doing that awkward almost-but-not-quite-jogging thing like I'm in a three-legged race. Wish I could move faster, but my body hurts too much.

"Justin!" Nia says. "Slow down."

One . . . two . . . three . . . Breathe. I can't get enough air.

I leap off the curb and start across the street.

What if our Zee is gone forever?

"Watch out!" Lyric says.

Gone like my mom.

A large white blur speeds toward me.

04

Lyric snags me around the waist and jerks me back onto the side-walk. I fall into his body and only his strong grip keeps me from eating the concrete.

Brakes screech as tires blacken the pavement right where I'd been standing. The smell of burning rubber fills the air. Smoke billows out from the back of a Sweet Dreams ice cream truck.

Whoa. That was close.

First Carla came to the party, then Zee attacked me, now I'm almost roadkill . . . My mom used to say any day above ground is a good day. Today is proving her wrong.

Nia pushes Lyric away and grabs my arm, giving me a firm

shake. "Don't scare me like that. You could be dead and I'd be sooooooo mad at you."

"Me too," says Lyric.

Hyde Miller, the neighborhood ice cream guy, jumps out of the open driver's-side door. His dad owns Sweet Dreams, but he just started to work there this summer.

"Hey." His mustardy-brown eyes slowly slither over me, from head to toe.

I cringe. A puffy scar zigzags from his right temple down to his chin. One hard tug might unzip his cheek. There are all kinds of stories about what happened—raccoon attack, shaving gone bad, knife fight in an alley, car accident. It's an unsolved mystery and there's no right way to ask why someone's face is jacked up.

Nia plants her hands on her hips. "Did you *just* get your license? You almost killed Justin." Her right foot tap, tap, taps a beat on the sidewalk. She's scary when she's angry. "Did you know the speed limit in a residential area is fifteen miles per hour?"

"There's a sign? Where?" Hyde tugs on the sleeves of his untucked shirt. He's wearing all black. He even has a leather glove on his left hand. He's dressed for a funeral or covert mission, not to sell ice cream.

"You need to be more careful," says Nia.

"He shouldn't run into the street without looking both ways. I could tell his mom," Hyde shoots back.

I wince.

Lyric's eyes cut to me and then he steps forward, glaring at Hyde. "Dude, you need to check yourself. What's up with the tattling threat? It was an accident." Lyric crosses his arms. "How about I tell your dad you're out here putting our lives in danger with your bad driving?"

Hyde's hands clench into fists at his sides. He glances down and mumbles to himself for a moment. Then his slumped shoulders pop back and he clears his throat. When he looks at me again, his eyes are eerily blank. "Sorry about that. Are you okay, kid?"

Kid? He's not *that* much older than us. Maybe around nineteen like my sister, Victoria, though he seems younger.

"I'm good." I wipe the sweat from my clammy forehead. "I shoulda been looking where I was going."

Nia's narrowed eyes run over me. I exhale a slow breath to calm my racing heart.

"You really okay?" she whispers.

I nod jerkily. That slight movement causes me to sway. Nia loops her arm through mine to steady me. Must breathe. Inhale. Exhale.

Hyde points a gloved finger toward Zee's house. "Y'all coming from there?"

"Pfft. If you were *paying attention,* you'd know where we were coming from," Nia says.

She's still not over it.

Hyde rolls his eyes. "I didn't get to meet Zee when I dropped off the cart. He's been in the news. I was hoping—"

"What?" Nia's eyes narrow. She looks Hyde up and down.

A muscle ticks in his jaw. His eyes are locked on Zee's house.

"Look, it was cool of you to deliver that ice cream, but Zee doesn't need any more drama," Lyric says. "He's been through a lot already and—"

"Stop being so nosey," Nia says while glaring at Hyde.

He holds up his hands. "Whoa, whoa, whoa. I heard some stuff and . . . Forget it. I wasn't gonna bother him."

My head is spinning. I tug my arm away from Nia and ease down onto the curb. I glance across the street. Two dogs and a cat stand side by side, staring in our direction. They're so still it's like they're not even real. They slowly back away. The hairs on the back of my neck stand up. What the—?

Nia peeks over her shoulder to check on me. I smile weakly. It's cool she tries to look out for me, but there's no hiding this is not my best moment. I glance back toward the weird animals and they're gone.

"So, is the party officially over? I'm not supposed to pick up my ice cream cart until six, but I can grab it now," says Hyde.

"Zee wasn't feelin' too good, so we rolled out a little early," says Lyric. "We had to stop mid-game. You might wanna wait and come back tomorrow to pick up your stuff."

Hyde's head jerks around so fast I hear his neck crack. "Game? You played a game?" he asks, his voice going from fake deep to high-pitched.

"Well . . ." Lyric rocks back on his heels. "We tried to play Hide and Seek, but—"

Hyde gasps. His face is a flipbook of emotions, changing so rapidly it's hard to keep track—excitement, fear, sadness, concern—all with that writhing scar. It's alarming.

The sky rumbles and a loud clap of thunder makes me jump.

"Dude, you okay?" Lyric takes a slow step away from Hyde.

Hyde shifts from foot to foot. His long, untied shoestrings dance across the ground. "I'm . . ." He stops as if he can't find the right words.

Dark clouds crawl across the sky. A sudden cool breeze chills my hot body.

"I gotta go." His haunted gaze travels from Lyric, Nia, then to me. He spins on his heels and jumps inside the ice cream truck. It takes him a couple of attempts before he gets it running. The truck jerks forward and glides away as a creepy jingle crackles to life. High-pitched kid voices cheerfully sing, "Eat ice cream and play. Eat ice cream and play. I scream, you scream. Eat ice cream and play." Then the kids scream and the song repeats.

"That's new music. I definitely would have remembered something that disturbing," says Nia.

"What just happened?" Lyric's dark freckles are the only color on his pale face.

"Today went from weird to weirder," says Nia.

I stand on wobbly legs. Time for me to roll out. "I'll catch y'all later." I need space. Not outdoor space, but the space of my small, safe room. I never shoulda left the house anyway, but I couldn't let Mrs. Murphy and Zee down. And look how that turned out.

"Wait, we need to talk about Zee," says Nia.

No, we don't. My head hurts just thinking about him.

"Yeah, what about all that stuff he said?" Lyric asks. "It sounded important. He was really scared. It was almost like he was trying to warn us."

"He's . . . he's . . ." What is he? Sick? Confused? Traumatized? All three. "It was probably nothing. Mrs. Murphy said he hasn't been sleeping good and—"

Lyric groans. "Aww, dude, don't turn around."

Of course, I have to look. A white van with Tennessee Water and Electric branding on the side is parked in front of my house. A woman with a clipboard stands on my front porch. I watch as she knocks repeatedly on the door. When no one answers, she peeks inside a window.

"Bill collector," says Lyric.

My eyes widen. "How do you know?"

"I recognize the signs," he says. "They're always rolling up to my house. Different companies, but there's always a white van and someone with a clipboard. I recognize that lady, too. She's stopped by my place a few times."

"That's not right," says Nia.

He shrugs. "People want their money. I hate when they just pop up, though. It's so much easier to dodge phone calls. Late afternoon and early evening are prime bill collection time. They expect people to be home. And it's Friday. She's trying to handle her business before the weekend."

I massage the back of my stiff neck. Lyric and Nia know things have been hard since my mom died, but I haven't shared all the bad financial stuff. I glance around to see if any neighbors are outside watching. Everyone will know our problems.

Lyric crosses his arms. "How do you want to play this? I'll back you up."

"There are options?" asks Nia.

"Oh yeah. We could hit her van with some water balloons. I have my slingshot. It's worked for me—"

"It's fine," I say quickly. "I'll handle it." Might as well deal with it now. She's only gonna come back another time. And I'm tired. I want to go home. I've had enough of running and hiding today.

I make a mental note to tell my counselor about this decision. She'll be happy I'm choosing to confront rather than avoid. This has to be progress.

Lyric and Nia exchange a glance, then she nudges me with her shoulder. "Sooo . . . call me later if you wanna talk or something."

I nod. I won't call.

She starts to say something, then stops herself.

Nia knows when to back off. It's one of the things I like best about her.

She turns to Lyric. "We're having spaghetti for dinner. There's plenty if you want to come over. Unless you have to get home?"

"Nawww." Lyric rocks back and forth on his heels. "My mom's kinda busy doing stuff tonight. I could work with noodles and sauce."

Lyric's mom works late, when she works at all. Since his folks aren't around, Nia and her parents make sure he has a place to eat and hang out.

"I just have to be home before dark," he says.

"Did you know there are more than six hundred shapes of pasta?" Nia asks.

Lyric turns to me, his eyebrows arched. I shrug. He's on his own now.

"I did not know that," he says as they walk away. "You're not gonna, uh, list them all, are you?"

She tugs him down the street.

He peeks over his shoulder. "Hey, we're still on for the mall tomorrow, right?"

I totally forgot about that. All I want to do is hide out in my house, but a while ago Lyric asked me to go check out instruments with him. "Yeah. Sure."

"Cool. And we can talk more about Zee," he yells back as they cut across an overgrown lawn and disappear around the tall oak trees lining the street.

The sky spits out raindrops, but I stay on the cracked sidewalk until my shirt becomes so damp it clings to my body. With one last look at Zee's hauntingly still house, I force myself to move.

As I walk down the sidewalk, a police car drives by again. They shoulda been patrolling when Zee went missing. I glare, but not openly, because that would be dumb.

I stop next to my tilted mailbox. If there was a contest for the most neglected house on the block, mine would win. The color is a dingy white, and the black shutters hang off the windows. Since Mom died, my sister, Victoria, and I have kinda let things go. Mom wouldn't like it, but it's not really home anymore. Not without her.

The utilities woman turns and freezes when she sees me in the driveway. Exhaling a deep breath, I walk toward her. She flicks her long, blond braid over her shoulder as she marches down the steps. Her face is red from the heat and the color matches the shirt tucked inside her dark jeans. Her clothing is casual, but her expression is all business.

She holds up the clipboard and there is a large sweat stain under her arm.

"You live here?" she asks.

"Yeah."

"Are your parents around?"

My jaw tightens. "I don't have any parents." My dad left a long time ago. He has a new wife and new kids. A new life. And my mom is dead.

The woman's eyes narrow. "So, you live here by yourself? There's no adult—"

"My older sister," I say quickly. The last thing I need is for her to file a report with some child agency saying I'm an unsupervised minor. "She's either at school or work. She'll be home later."

"Well . . ." She studies the papers on her clipboard. "I need to speak to an adult about some billing concerns."

I swallow hard and remain silent. I'm clearly not an adult so I don't know what to tell her. Maybe she'll just leave so Victoria and I can come up with a plan to deal with this.

The woman sighs. "Look, I'm not supposed to do this since you're unsupervised, but it's Friday and I want to go home and I have to turn in my weekly report."

She tugs some papers off her clipboard. "This is your bill." She hands them to me.

I stare at the document. My eyes widen. "One thousand eight hundred fifty-four dollars," I whisper. We're that far behind?

Once Mom's savings ran out, we fell behind on our bills. We still haven't recovered.

The woman shifts from foot to foot. She glances at a laminated card taped to her clipboard. "At Tennessee Water and Electric, we understand that sometimes customers fall behind on their bills due to unexpected and inconvenient circumstances."

My hand clenches, crumbling the papers. I wonder what category my mom's death would fall under. Unexpected or inconvenient?

"We want to work with you to keep your energy costs down, and help you manage your bill. Ending your service is always the last resort, as this would make it difficult to later reinstate your account," she reads.

No electricity. No water. We can't live here if they turn everything off. What would we do? Where would we go? I blink hard. The woman is blurry. Inhale. Exhale. Chest burns.

"Are you okay?" she asks.

I stagger past her and onto my porch. My trembling fingers fumble with the door lock and after several tries I'm able to get inside. My breath is loud in my ears.

I slam the door closed. The world tilts back and forth as I stumble down the hall and into my room. I bump my nightstand and a puzzle box falls to the floor, scattering pieces all around me. Gasping, I fall forward onto my bed and a defeated cry erupts out of me.

Everything is so messed up! I ball up the bill and hurl it across the room. One thousand eight hundred fifty-four dollars. I punch my pillow. Carla's face swims through my vision. My fist pounds the pillow again. Zee's chant rings in my ears. He's supposed to be my friend, but he's different now. Scary. The real Zee might never come back. Punch, punch, punch.

Sweat trickles down my face. If my mom were here, she'd know what to do. She'd make everything better, but she's gone. Everybody leaves. Nothing stays the same. Nothing fits anymore.

"I wish I could disappear." I rub my chest and gaze at the picture next to the baseball trophies on my dresser. My mom's smiling and healthy face stares back at me. What would she think if she saw me like this? She wanted me to be strong, but I'm not. "I'm sorry, Mom." My voice cracks.

Time ticks away as I finally regain control. So much for my month-long record of no major panic attacks. With a weary sigh, I climb off the bed and, one by one, place the puzzle pieces back inside the box. Landscapes and space scenes were my favorite, but my mom loved the wildlife and food designs. Every night, even when she was sick, we'd work on a different puzzle. We completed all of them except . . .

I tug the piece from my pocket and stare at it. It's blue and orange. A tiny portion of the sun setting behind a mountain. I press it to my heart. Mom. Three hundred and ninety-seven days.

Eventually, exhaustion swallows me up. I crawl back into my bed, determined to forget today. As I drift into a restless sleep, Zee's creepy words overtake me, almost as if he's whispering in my ear. In some deep corner of my mind I realize this isn't Zee's voice.

"Now it's my time to seek and play. New rules you'll have to learn and obey. Get ready for mischief to begin. One by one, until I win. Tonight begins the game of sorrow. The fears begin when you wake tomorrow."

05

"No!" I jerk awake and fight off the tangled sheets, panting. I scramble back until I slam against the bed frame. My blurry eyes zoom around. I'm in my room. Safe. Bright beams of sunlight shoot through the blinds, forming a cage around my bed.

Images from my freaktastic nightmare flash through my head before fading away—darkness, cold, a feeling of being trapped and unable to breathe. I shiver and tug at my T-shirt stuck to my sticky skin.

"Zee." I collapse against my headboard. This is his fault—all those creepy threats. He got into my head. Stop it! Not gonna think about him or yesterday. Today will be better. It definitely can't be worse. I wipe the sweat off my face and glance at the clock on the nightstand: 11:56 a.m. I slept for a long time, but it doesn't feel like it. And no matter how much I want to rest some more, I can't. Too much to do. Like figure out how we're gonna pay the bills.

With a weary groan, I roll out of bed and rummage through a pile of semi-clean clothes on the floor. I pull on the first thing my hands touch and shove my feet into ratty kicks. Should probably shower but I'm already dressed and we need to save money on the water bill anyway. Besides, Lyric won't care if I smell a little. Hope he doesn't keep me in the mall all day and really hope he won't talk about Zee the whole time.

After quickly brushing my teeth and washing the crust from my eyes in my small bathroom, I grab my puzzle piece off my nightstand and stuff it in my back pocket. I open the door and step into the hall. The house is deadly quiet, which means Victoria is gone—again. With school and her work schedule, I hardly see her.

I hurry past my mom's bedroom. Its day 398. I switch on the television in the living room to drown out the count echoing in my head.

I enter the kitchen and grab a bowl of cereal. A high-pitched tone blares from the television. Beep. Beep. Beep. I peek around the corner. The monitor is white and a message scrolls across the bottom of the screen in large black letters.

ALERT, ALERT, ALERT. MISSING . . . SHAE DAVIDSON, FROM BOYLE HEIGHTS, AGE TEN. PLEASE CONTACT YOUR

LOCAL POLICE DEPARTMENT WITH ANY INFORMATION. ALERT, ALERT, ALERT.

The spoon slips from my fingers. Milk splashes all over my face. Shae's school photo appears onscreen. She's smiling in front of a forest backdrop with her hands folded on a tree stump. Several other pictures appear—Shae in a ballet outfit onstage, Shae in one of those kid pageant things, Shae in a pink bedroom, surrounded by dolls.

I set my bowl down and it misses the counter. Crash. I dash into the living room and slide to a halt inches from the television. Channel Nine News reporter Misty Morgan appears. Her blond helmet of hair fills most of the screen, but I can see a line of news vans parked in the background.

"I'm reporting live from outside the house of Rosiland and Carl Davidson, whose ten-year-old daughter, Shae, disappeared yesterday, around three in the afternoon, from the Lake Winnepesaukah campgrounds. A frantic search is currently underway to find this precious little girl," Misty says with a thick Southern accent.

"What?" I shout at the screen. "That can't be right, she—"

"Shae was last seen with members of her dance team after a performance at the camp. Police and volunteers have organized a search party and are currently conducting interviews with Lake Winnie counselors and Shae's fellow campers. I'm here with Mrs. Davidson to find out how she's dealing with this horrific situation."

Shae's mom steps forward. Her hair is pointing in every direction and tears pour from her swollen eyes. She grabs the Channel Nine News mic from Misty's manicured hands. "Whoever you are, please bring back my precious baby. We love her so much. I'll do anything. Pay any amount. *Please.* I love my daughter." Mrs. Davidson falls to her knees, wailing.

The camera cuts away, then refocuses on Misty Morgan, who winces. She leans down and retrieves the mic. "As you can see, Mrs. Davidson is clearly distraught and the community is in shock," says Misty. "This is the second child to vanish from this area, but thankfully Zechariah Murphy was found safe after his mysterious year-long disappearance from Kidz Art Kamp. We can only hope and pray Shae will return much sooner than that. If anyone has information that can help, please contact the police. Back to you in the station, Rob." She smiles, somberly, flashing unnaturally white teeth.

I switch off the television. What is going on? The news is saying Shae disappeared around three from Lake Winnepesaukah, but that's over a two-hour drive from here. Zee's party was at four and Shae was there. I *saw* her. *Talked* to her. It doesn't make any sense.

There's a sudden flash of movement in the corner of my eye and I spin around. The living room is still—scuffed hardwoods, popcorn ceiling, dusty furniture, dying plants. Nothing seems out of place, but . . . someone just walked over my grave.

That's what my mom used to call that creepy feeling you get

when you know something is wrong, but don't know exactly what it is.

KNOCK, KNOCK, KNOCK. The front door rattles on its hinges. I stumble back, hitting my leg on the edge of the coffee table. "Owww."

"Justin," a voice yells.

Heart pounding, I exhale a shaky breath. It's Nia.

I limp across the room and fling the door open. Nia stands on the porch, and behind her is Quincy, wearing his school backpack. Why is he here?

Nia pushes past me, pulling Quincy inside after her. She throws herself onto the couch. Quincy flops down on a chair. He clutches his backpack to his chest.

"Did you hear about Shae?" Nia asks.

"Shae," Quincy repeats sadly.

"I just saw it on the news." I rub my throbbing leg. "They said she was away at dance camp, but—"

"What's that about? I mean, we saw her, right? Didn't we?" Nia is practically shouting.

Her borderline panic rubs off on me, and I quickly replay yesterday over in my mind. Yes, Shae was definitely there. She was the one who suggested Hide and Seek.

"It doesn't make sense," Nia says. "And guess what . . . Carla is missing, too." She points at Quincy. He nods once.

I swallow hard. "What?!"

"I ran into him on the way here. He was running away to search for his sister."

"What do you mean?" I'm about to lose it.

Quincy's mouth opens and closes. Opens. Closes.

Nia springs forward and shakes him. "Use your words. Use your words."

"Uh, Carla wasn't around when I woke up and I can't find her."

"But Misty Morgan didn't say anything about Carla." I lean against the arm of a chair since my legs won't hold me.

Quincy lowers his head. His shoulders touch his ears. "My parents think she ran off. She does that sometimes, but she tells me first and she's usually back after a few hours. And she, uh, left something. She would never take off without it."

"Justin, we were with them yesterday and now they're gone." Nia bites her lip. "What if we need to be interrogated by the police? Should we turn ourselves in?" She gasps. "What if we're suspects?"

"Whoa, whoa, whoa." I hold up my hands. "We didn't do anything." Did we? Oh man, my brain is fried.

"What if some psycho is targeting kids in our neighborhood?" Nia whimpers. "You put up all those missing flyers for Zee and created that website so people could post if they saw something. Are we gonna have to do that for Carla now, for Shae?"

No, this is different. It has to be. "Quincy, where would Carla go? Did she say anything?"

He scratches the back of his neck. "Well, uh, she was pretty mad about the party, you know, with Zee and everything. She said it was his fault she got bit."

"Bit?"

"She got a mark on her wrist last night, like a bad sore. She said she must have gotten it when she hid under the porch."

"How is that Zee's fault?" Nia asks.

Quincy shrugs.

"What did it look like?" I say.

"It was bumpy and swirly." Quincy's thick eyebrows meet in the middle as he thinks. "Like a cinnamon roll."

"That sounds like ringworm," says Nia. "Gross."

"No, it was different." Quincy shifts on the chair, setting his backpack on the floor next to his feet. "Carla said it burned real bad, and it felt like something was, uh, moving under her mark."

I rub the back of my tense neck. A mark. Why does that sound so familiar?

"What?" Nia asks me. "What is it?"

Startled, I turn to her. "It's just . . . Nothing."

"No, not nothing," says Nia, pointing a finger at me. "What are you thinking?"

I run a shaky hand over my face. "You remember when Zee flipped out? He kept repeating that weird chant. 'Out of the darkness, no more light, now it comes to steal your life.' Then he mentioned something about a *mark*. What if—"

"It wasn't a bite?" Nia says with wide eyes. "What would that mark mean?"

"Look, it's stupid. Forget it. Nothing scary is happening." I don't sound as convincing as I want to.

Quincy slowly raises his hand like he's in school and wants the teacher to call on him.

"Yes, Quincy," Nia says.

"Last night, did anyone have a bad dream? Like hear something say weird stuff?"

"What kind of stuff?" *Please don't let it be the same, please don't let it be the same.*

Quincy swallows hard. "Now it's my time to seek and play. New rules you'll have to learn and obey. Get ready for mischief to begin. One by one, until I win."

"I had a nightmare and heard the same scary words," Nia whispers and hugs herself.

I sink onto the couch. This is bad. Real bad. "How is that possible?"

"Did Zee curse us or something?" asks Quincy.

My mom used to say, "When it rains, it pours." That means that when bad stuff happens, more and more bad stuff happens. She was right. I'm drowning in a sea of scary.

"Let's go." Nia jumps to her feet, grabs Quincy by the arm, and tugs him toward the door.

"Wait! My backpack!" he cries.

It's on the floor next to the chair. He races back to get it and tugs it onto his shoulders.

"You too," she says to me.

"Go? Go where?" I'm fine right here. Inside. Not searching for trouble.

"To see Zee. We need answers," she says with her "duh" face.

I shake my head. Nope. Not going back over there. Doesn't she remember what happened yesterday? Zee could be dangerous and I hate seeing him so . . . different.

Nia pushes Quincy out the door and turns to glare at me. Chin out. Hands on hips. Foot tapping to her own frantic beat. Not good.

"We need to find out what's going on," Nia says. "Do you want to just sit around and wait for something bad to happen? What if something happens to me while I'm out looking for answers? Would you be happy you stayed home then? I sure don't want anything bad happening to you."

"Nia, I—"

"You're my very best friend and I love you. Not love love, 'cause that would be gross, but I do care about you. We've known each other since we were born. You never forget about me and you always listen to me even when you don't want to. You *hear* me." She tugs on my right ear.

I blink. Blink again. She's talking so fast I only catch every other word.

"We're so close it's like we're related. Wait! That would be so cool! Victoria could be my big sister, too. She's way cooler than my two brothers. Maybe we should have a DNA test. Did you know DNA stands for deoxyribonucleic acid and—"

"Okay, okay, okay. Let's go." I'll do anything to make her stop talking. "But I want to say this is the stupidest, craziest, worst idea ever." Just putting it out there so she can't get mad when I yell, "I told you so." Which I will, if this goes bad. I have no shame.

"Cool." Her sudden smile goes from ear to ear. She flips her braids over her shoulders and marches off.

My eyes narrow. I've been played. Well done, Nia. Well done.

The moment I step outside, the humidity punches me in the face. Even though the gray clouds have stolen most of the sunlight, it's so hot I immediately start sweating. Glad I didn't bother with a shower. Woulda been a waste of time and water.

My steps falter as I jog down my driveway. Something feels off, like something has shifted though I can't figure out what. A tan cat bolts from under a car and scurries up a tree. From a high branch, it hisses at me and cowers against the tree trunk. Weird.

I take my time catching up with Nia and Quincy. He stares up the road, his shoulders slumped. I'm no fan of Carla, but she's his sister and best friend. Now she's gone and we have no idea what happened to her. It's like Zee all over again.

Nia pats him on the back and whispers something in his ear. He nods and stands up straighter. She's good with people, with being supportive and stuff. Every kid should have at least one friend as awesome as Nia.

As we cross the street, steam hisses from the manholes, blanketing the area with an eerie fog. The spooky atmosphere magnifies my sense of doom as we walk up Zee's front porch steps. The welcome home decorations look even sadder than they did yesterday.

Nia knocks on the door; it drifts open with a bloodcurdling squeak. We stand in the doorway and stare inside.

Nia gasps.

The coffee table is overturned and its broken legs dangle from exposed nails. There are small, fist-shaped holes in the wall. A mound of dirt is the final resting place of an uprooted plant. A lamp hangs off the side of the tilted couch by its tangled cord. The screen on the television is shattered.

A chill slides down my spine. "Oh man."

"Who did this?" Quincy whispers.

"Mrs. Murphy? Zee?" Nia's voice quivers as she starts forward.

My hand trembles as I grab her arm. "Wait. We can't go in there." This is the classic what-not-to-do scenario in every scary movie.

"Police." Quincy backs away, pulling on my free arm.

Yeah. What he said.

"What if someone's hurt? We need to help," says Nia.

"Let's help from across the street. With a phone call," I say.

Quincy tugs on my arm. I tighten my grip on Nia. We're a human chain.

"Hey! Let go!" Nia squirms.

"No way." I pull her back. "We are not going—"

"Not you," cries Nia.

A hand grips her other wrist. Before I can react, we're yanked forward into the house and I pull Quincy along with me. The door slams shut behind us.

06

I scream and almost faint. Not even gonna lie.

Quincy falls to the floor, curling into a tight ball. He rolls into the nearest corner.

Nia's turbo-charged arms and legs windmill and kick at a dizzying speed. "Get away from me. I will hurt you. I know kung fu, karate, and jujitsu. I will tae kwon do you up in here!"

"Hey, watch the face," a voice cries. "Chill out! It's just me."

"Lyric?!"

He lowers his arms from where he's covering his head. I don't know whether to hug or choke him. "Man, what are you doing here?"

Nia slaps his arm. "You scared me to death. You're talking to a ghost." She extends her arms and walks stiffly in a circle. "Boooo."

Lyric tilts his head to the side and studies her. "That's more zombie-like, but I get where you're going."

Quincy scrambles to his feet, stumbling over the furniture.

"What happened?" Nia gestures to the broken table.

"Zee," says Lyric with a heavy sigh. "Mrs. Murphy said he tried to leave last night. He kept talking about stopping something. Apparently, it was a rough night."

"Is she okay?" I ask.

Lyric nods. "Yeah. She needed to run to the store to get stuff for Zee and asked if I'd hang here until she got back. Zee's in his room resting. I was cleaning up some, then thought I'd go check on him but y'all showed up."

Lyric sweeps the trash into a dustpan. Half-hidden under the broken leaves is a harmonica. He picks it up and shakes off the dirt. Small pieces of newspaper and tape are still stuck to one dented side. It's Zee's welcome home gift.

Lyric swallows hard and his hand clenches around the harmonica.

Nia steps forward. "Lyric—"

"It's cool. I can fix it or get him another one," he says.

The harmonica may have come from a thrift store, but it cost something. Lyric doesn't have extra money to waste. He saved up a long time for that gift and now it's busted.

I look around the room again and this overwhelming need to run and hide hits me with such force I have to catch my breath. I take a step toward the door, putting a little more distance between me and Zee's room. Why did he want to leave so badly? Where was he going?

"Did you hear about Shae?" Nia asks.

Lyric nods. "Yeah, it's all over my police scanner."

Wait, what? "You have a police scanner?"

Lyric shrugs. "It was my dad's. It helped him know things."

"What kind of things?" I ask.

Nia snaps her fingers at us. "Focus, please. The news said Shae was at a dance camp that's two hours away, but she was at the party with us. What's up with that?"

"It's not possible," says Lyric. "She couldn't be in two places at once."

"Maybe she's with Carla," Quincy says.

Lyric's eyebrows rise. "Carla? Why would Shae be with her? And what's up with the backpack?"

Quincy tugs on the straps. "Uh . . . I have stuff for Carla."

"Carla disappeared, too." The words tumble from my mouth. "She's gone."

Lyric's jaw drops. "Nuh-uh. Like ran off or missing missing?"

Quincy's eyes are so wide they've combined. He's a cyclops.

"Which one?" Lyric asks him. "Ran off or missing missing?"

Quincy stares blindly. We've lost him.

"Missing missing." It's easier if I answer.

"Go ahead and freak out. I already did." Nia slumps against the overturned couch.

"Whoa. I mean, whoa." Lyric bites his thumbnail. "Carla? And this stuff about Shae . . . Dude."

"There's something else." I swallow hard. "We were talking at my place . . . Did you have a nightmare last night? Hear a freaky voice?"

His blue eyes widen. "Man, yeah! It was bad. Something was like stalking me and saying weird stuff. Might not ever sleep again. And when I woke up that scary feeling was still there." He touches his chest. "Like inside me."

"We had the same dream." Nia tugs at her braids. "And I feel different, too. Not right."

Quincy nods. "Me too."

"What's going on?" asks Nia.

Their eyes lock on me. Whoa. Hold up. "Why is everybody lookin' at me?"

"What do we do?" Lyric asks.

"Run. Hide." Quincy eases toward the door.

"I kinda agree with Quincy." I can't believe those words came out of my mouth.

"No, you don't," says Nia.

"I don't?" I ask.

Lyric crosses his arms and stares at me intensely. "You always have a plan. You're our official unofficial leader. Lead."

I study my sneakers. I might have been the leader in the past, but we've never faced anything like this. How am I supposed to figure out why all this strange stuff is happening? Anyway, that was the old me, the pre-Mom-death me. Things are different now. *I'm* different now.

"Justin, we have to figure out what's happening and find Carla and Shae. What if we're next? I'm not down with disappearing," says Nia.

My shoulders slump. "Okay, look, since we're already here, we might as well talk to Zee. He said some strange stuff yesterday and he was really upset. Maybe he knows something."

Lyric's bushy eyebrows bounce up his forehead. "Like he's involved? Zee? How? Why? No way."

"Well . . ." Nia fidgets with a button on her shirt. "It did sorta sound like he was threatening us."

Even after everything that went down yesterday, I don't wanna believe Zee would hurt anybody; he's my friend. Well, he used to be. "Any other ideas?" Please. Someone. Anything?

Nia's lips screw from left to right. She taps her chin. Quincy stares at the wall.

Lyric scratches the side of his head. "I got nothing."

"Me either," says Nia.

Great. No help. I march down the hall. "Let's hurry before Mrs. Murphy gets back."

We stop outside Zee's room. Nia gasps and points at the locks on the door. "Ooooooh."

"Yeah, that's what I thought when I saw the locks," says Lyric.

Quincy glances down the hall like he's about to make a break for it. "I'll wait outside."

Nia grabs his arm. "We should stay together."

"I wish Carla was here," he whispers, his voice trembling.

"That's why we need to talk to Zee," I say. "To see if he knows how to help find her." I place my ear against the door and listen for a sound that screams DO NOT ENTER, but I only hear my loud breathing.

Nia's warm breath tickles the tiny hairs on the back of my neck. "What are you waiting for?"

Personal boundaries—none. We need to discuss that later.

My tongue skims across my dry lips as my numb fingers release the dead bolts. Click. Click. Click. With a slight push, the door glides open with a loud whine. Cold air whooshes from the room and chills my skin. I'm hit with the strong smell of fresh paint and markers.

"Whoaaaaaa," says Lyric.

The bedroom walls used to be filled with Zee's cool artwork—drawings of superheroes and robots. Now the paintings are covered with large splashes of black paint, numbers, and strange symbols. The movie posters, life-size creature standees, and action figures are gone. His desk, bookshelf, and television are missing. Instead there's a twin mattress on the floor with a mountain of tangled blankets.

The only light comes from the bulb hanging from the ceiling and the rays of sunlight that have wrestled past the paint-splattered blinds.

A whimper breaks the stunned silence. My gaze flies across the room to the huddled figure rocking back and forth in a corner. Markers, paper, paintbrushes, and other art supplies are scattered around him. Zee stares at a wall as if hypnotized.

"He's been in here alone like this?" whispers Lyric. "This room . . . it's like his prison. This ain't right."

Nia nudges me toward Zee. "Go talk to him."

I dig my heels into the floor. "Why me?"

Nia pokes me. I spin around and grab her finger. She tugs. I tug harder and glare at her. She growls. Stare off.

Lyric swats his hands at us. "Dude, can you two stop?! We need to hurry. Mrs. Murphy could be back any minute."

"We'll all go," Nia says.

Good idea. We shuffle into the room as one, like we're stuck together with Velcro. We tremble. It could be from the cold, but my vote is that it's from fear.

"Zee." My voice cracks. "We, uh, want to ask you about yesterday."

No response.

"Carla and Shae are missing," I tell him.

Still nothing.

"Zee." Lyric holds up the broken harmonica. "Look, man. Don't worry about this. I'll get you a new one." He hesitantly lifts it to his mouth and plays a little tune. The sound is so spookily off-key, I flinch.

Lyric stops playing and stares at the instrument for a long moment. "You can keep this one for now, just in case you want to start practicing," he says to Zee.

Nia squeezes my hand as Lyric slides the harmonica across the scuffed hardwood floor. It lands near Zee's leg but he still doesn't respond. He continues to stare at a drawing of a big insect-like creature. Its head is grotesquely large and its face is covered with red eyes—no nose, no mouth. Zee has drawn thin arms with scales extending from the body and its hands are sharp claws. The wings protruding from its back are black with spikes. It looks horrifying and creepily realistic.

"This was a bad idea," I say. "Let's—"

Zee leaps to his feet and turns to face us. We scramble back, slamming into the wall with a loud group thud.

He stalks across the room. He's even paler than yesterday and the scars on his arms stand out even more.

"Justin," says Nia shakily. "Look at his wrist."

There's a swirl pattern, slightly bigger than a quarter.

"That's the mark. That's what Carla had on her arm," Quincy says.

I swallow the lump in my throat. "Zee?"

Tears trickle down his cheeks. He holds out a photo. His fingers are stained from the black and red markers.

The picture was taken after a baseball game two years ago. Zee was on my team and we won first place in the tournament. He's holding the trophy. My arm is around his neck as I playfully have him in a headlock.

That was one of my last good memories. A month later I learned my mom was sick. Zee had my back like always. He spent more time at my house than his own. He helped me deal with everything and even took care of my mom on the days I couldn't, when it was too hard for me to see her so sick.

Lyric and Nia were there for me, too, but it was different. They wanted to cheer me up, make me feel better. They promised it would all be okay, but Zee didn't. He didn't say much at all. He let me freak out. He listened when I needed to talk and some nights he sat silently watching while me, my mom, and Victoria worked on our puzzles.

Then he disappeared, and a week later Mom died. I lost them both. I stare at the photo. We're both so different now.

"I couldn't do it," he says.

My eyes fly back to his face. For a brief moment, I see my friend. All of him.

He extends his fist. His thin arm trembles. I hesitantly bump his knuckles with mine. "Zee, I don't understand. Do what?"

"Play. I said I would . . . but I couldn't . . ." A shade falls over his eyes and his nostrils flare. He hits his head with his fist. "I—I—I didn't do my part." A knot bulges in his throat as if the words are stuck. "Want to help. Want to help." He growls. "I didn't mean it. Bad place. Had to leave. Sorry, sorry, sorry."

And just like that, he's gone. Lost again. My heart burns a hole through my chest.

I nudge Nia back toward the door.

"Zee, what happened to Carla and Shae?" Lyric asks.

"Are we in danger?" Nia asks. "What does that mark mean?"

She tries to get around me, but I hold her back.

Zee walks back toward his weird wall. "I went up the hill, the hill was muddy, stomped my toe and made it bloody. Out of the darkness, no more light, the Seeker comes to steal your life. Yesterday you sealed your fate, by playing what it loves to hate. Once you're tagged, then you'll know. The mark appears, it's your time to go. Now you're in the final count. It's closer to the set amount. Once it reaches its final goal, with the power that it stole, it will win and now can roam. Our world becomes its seeking home."

That's it. We're out! I shove everyone into the hallway. As I close the door, Lyric's hand shoots out. "Wait. What's he doing?"

Zee grabs a large black marker off the floor and draws five stick figures on the wall. He's an awesome artist, but this looks like something a toddler would draw.

His motion is jerky and frantic. He writes names above each

figure. Carla. Quincy. Nia. Lyric. Justin. Then with a giant X, he crosses out each person.

Quincy makes a sound—a combo of a screech, moan, and laugh. Is that a hit list?

Nia gasps. "What—"

"Game over, Justin," Zee says. "It's my fault it came. Now you'll pay. Now you'll pay. Now you'll pay." He waves the marker around wildly. "You're here, you're not, to that place you'll go. You disappear and only fear you'll know."

I'm yanked from the room. Quincy slams the door.

Lyric locks the deadbolts. "What was that? He—"

BAM. THUD. The bedroom door shakes like he's slamming himself against it. The doorknob turns.

Quincy races down the hallway faster than the Flash.

BAM! THUD! BAM! THUD!

Nia trips over her feet as she backs away. "What's he doing?"

BAM! BAM!

I gulp. "Trying to break through the door."

Wood around the doorframe splinters.

07

"Go!" I shove Nia and Lyric down the hallway. We dash out of the house, leap off the porch, and race down the driveway. On the sidewalk, we skid to a halt next to Quincy, who is doubled over with his arms wrapped around his middle. Panting, Lyric and Nia collapse on the lawn while I stand, ready to escape if Zee pulls a jailbreak and those locks don't hold.

Lyric wipes an arm across his damp forehead. "Did that just happen? Was he gonna hurt us? And what was he saying? It was like he was threatening us with some bad rap lyrics. He did the same thing at his party."

I don't know how to answer any of those questions. Crossing

out our names like that and trying to break down the door . . .

"Po . . . po . . . police." Quincy gasps for air.

"They don't care about the truth." Lyric's jaw clenches. "Remember what they did to my dad?"

Two years ago, Mr. Rivers, Lyric's dad, was hanging with some friends outside a convenience store. There was an argument and the police were called. Mr. Rivers was accused of resisting arrest and hitting a police officer. According to Lyric's dad, it was an accident. He was actually trying to break up the fight, and the officer got in the way. No one believed him, and Lyric's family didn't have extra money for a good lawyer. Mr. Rivers was sentenced to three years in prison.

"No police." Lyric's bright eyes plead with me to back him up.

"What would we say to them anyway? Our unstable friend is threatening us with some spooky stuff and drawing creepy artwork on his wall?" I ask with a little nod at Lyric. He mimics my movement. It's all good.

Nia fans herself with her long braids. "Okay, that does sound unbelievable and I don't want Zee to get into trouble."

"I feel ya, but it's kinda hard to be all 'Team Zee' right now," Lyric says.

Caw! Caw! Those stupid crows are back, circling above like we're dead meat they're about to feast on. Their wings slap at the air as they land on the roof. Their shadows glide over us, like they're tagging us with their creepiness. That odd sensation I had earlier is back, only stronger. It's not just the birds that are hovering, it's something else. Something I can't describe.

"Bad luck," I mutter with a shudder.

Lyric stands and brushes the grass off his jeans. "What are you talking about?"

"So much bad stuff happened yesterday. I—"

"Owww!" Quincy cries and grabs his arm. He stares down at his wrist.

"What? What's wrong?" Nia asks.

"It burns."

A swirl pattern appears on his skin. I suck in a loud breath.

Quincy hops around, swinging his arm. "It hurts!"

Nia grabs him. "Hold still. Let us see it."

I tug at my hair and spin around. "Oh man, oh man . . ." A mark. A mark.

"We saw that on Zee," Lyric says, pointing at Quincy's trembling arm. "What's going on?"

"Carla had a mark like that, too, before she disappeared," Nia explains faintly.

"Once you're tagged, then you'll know. The mark appears, it's your time to go," I repeat Zee's words.

Lyric frowns, then his jaw drops. "You think . . ." He looks at Quincy's arm. "We're . . . He . . . Oh man!"

"What's happening?" Quincy jerks his arm back. "What does this mean?"

"Justin, you're scaring me," Nia says.

I'm scaring myself. Suddenly every moment from Zee's party flashes through my mind. The memories shift and snap together like puzzle pieces. He wasn't talking nonsense. Those strange riddles were a threat and a *warning.*

"Okay, okay. Time out!" Lyric says, forming a "T" with his hands. "I need somebody to break this down for me. Are you saying that mark means we're gonna disappear? Carla was first and now it's gonna be Quincy?"

"I don't wanna disappear," he cries. "What did I do?"

"We're not guilty of anything." Lyric folds his arms.

I rub my aching temples. "It doesn't make any sense, but something is happening. And Zee made it seem like we're all involved."

"Are you thinking someone is after us?" Nia asks.

Lyric paces. "Like who? Why?"

"I don't know," I say.

Lyric releases a growl of frustration. "So we just wait and see if Quincy disappears and if we get tagged?"

"Where would I go?" Quincy shifts his backpack from one shoulder to the other. "Would I be with Carla and Shae?"

"There has to be something we can do. Someone who can help us figure this out," says Nia.

"Not Zee, clearly," I mumble. "But this all started with him."

"What do you mean?" Lyric asks.

"Zee was gone over a year. And we don't know anything about

what happened to him. And now other kids we know are disappearing. That can't be a coincidence." I glance back at Zee's house. Yesterday I stood in almost this exact spot talking myself into attending Zee's party. I wanted to support him, cheer him up. So much has changed in the last twenty-four hours.

I wish I could rewind time and change the past. All of it—keep Zee safe, take better care of my mom, be a better friend, son, brother. I can't fix what's already done, but maybe I can stop what could happen.

"We need to start from the beginning," I say.

Nia frowns. "What do you mean?"

"We need to talk to Zee's roommate from that art camp. Rodrigo. Remember, the news report said he was the last one to see Zee."

"Yeah, but he already talked to the police," Nia says. "They said they interviewed everyone from the camp."

Lyric snorts. "That doesn't mean anything. I wouldn't tell them everything, especially if it sounded cray-cray. He could have been worried they'd think he did something to Zee. How do we find Rodrigo?"

"I got this." Nia whips her phone out of her back pocket. "Did you know—"

Quincy drops his head in his hands. Lyric and I groan.

She continues like she didn't hear us. "Approximately sixty-nine percent of eleven- to fourteen-year-olds have their own cell phones, which have internet, which means social media, which means I can probably find him easy, 'cause I'm good like that."

"She's your friend," I jokingly say to Lyric.

Nia's fingers fly across the phone keys.

"Hey, heads up," Lyric says, staring over my shoulder.

I spin around as Mrs. Murphy pulls into her driveway. She parks and quickly climbs out of the car with a large grocery bag. "What's going on? Everything okay?" Her clothes are wrinkled and her messy hair is half up, half down.

Nia hides the phone behind her back. "Uh, we stopped by to check on Zee—"

"I told them he was asleep and we shouldn't bother him," Lyric says. He's so smooth even I buy the lie.

Mrs. Murphy hugs the bag close. "Maybe y'all can come back in a couple of days. I'm sure he'll be better then."

"Sure. No problem." I feel bad. Bad that Zee is messed up and she can't help him. Bad she has no idea what's going on; heck, we don't either. Bad she's so worn out. Bad I can't make it better like I wanted to do for my mom. Bad, bad, bad.

She walks up the front porch steps and hesitates at the door. "I really am sorry about what happened at the party. Zechariah's not himself, but he'd never deliberately hurt anybody."

"We know," says Nia.

"Will you tell Carla I'm sorry if she was scared by his behavior?"

Out the corner of my eye, I see Quincy flinch.

"We will." I lick my dry lips. There's something else I need to figure out. "And we'll tell Shae, too. That, uh, Zee's sorry." My heart thuds in my chest as I wait for Mrs. Murphy's response.

"Shae Davidson? The little girl from around the corner? I heard she's missing." Mrs. Murphy's eyes glaze over. "Her family must be heartbroken. I remember when Zechariah . . ." She falls silent and then focuses back on me. "Why would he apologize to Shae?"

I take a shaky step forward. "Didn't you invite her to the party yesterday?"

Mrs. Murphy's forehead creases. "No. Just you, Nia, Lyric, Carla, and Quincy."

"Not Shae Davidson?" Nia asks slowly, coming to stand next to me.

"No. Why do you ask?" Mrs. Murphy shifts her bag, using her knee to lift it more securely in her arms.

"Just wondering," I say with a weak smile.

There's a loud crash, like glass shattering from inside the house. Mrs. Murphy jumps. "I need to go." She rushes inside and closes the door.

"Bye, Mrs. Murphy," I whisper. The words taste sour in my mouth. I've got a horrible feeling I might not see her for a while.

"Whoa, whoa, whoa," Lyric says. "So Shae wasn't even invited *and* she was supposedly somewhere else at the same time?"

"But . . . but . . . it *was* Shae," says Quincy. "She looked pretty in her dance clothes."

Shae doesn't have a twin sister, but someone who looked, talked, and dressed like her came to Zee's welcome home party.

"If that wasn't the real Shae . . . ?" Nia bites her bottom lip.

Who or what *was it?*

08

Nia is scary good and found Rodrigo's address. His neighborhood is three miles away, so after we retrieve our bikes we head out.

With each push on my pedals I question this decision. What if Rodrigo doesn't know anything? This will be a wasted trip and we'll still have no answers. What if Rodrigo does have information, but it's bad? What do we do then? Can we stop whatever is happening before someone else disappears?

"Are we there yet?" Quincy says, leaning over his handlebars.

I glance over at him. He's breathing loudly and working hard not to fall behind. He's not the most athletic kid, but this short ride shouldn't be affecting him so much. He looks drained. There are dark circles under his puffy eyes. His brown skin has a slightly grayish tint. Is it the stress? The fear? Is it the mark on his wrist? I'm on question overload. My brain is about to explode.

"We're close," Nia says.

Quincy groans. A while ago, I offered to carry his backpack but he refused. I'm not sure if there's important stuff inside or if it's his safety net, like my puzzle piece. I get needing to have something you can trust, something you can hold on to for comfort.

As we make the right turn into Rodrigo's neighborhood a police car cruises by, then slows. The officer waves for us to stop. Great. What now?

"You kids aren't from around here." His thick mustache completely covers his top lip.

"What gave us away? The bikes?" Lyric asks.

I groan.

"Watch that attitude, kid." Officer Moustache raises his sunglasses to rest on top of his bald head and stares down Lyric.

Lyric doesn't even blink. Yeah, this could go bad fast.

"We're visiting a friend," Nia says quickly to diffuse the tense situation.

"His name is Rodrigo," adds Quincy.

"Huh," the officer says.

What does that mean? His eyes are hard, not cold and blank like Not-Shae, but still intense enough to make my heart stutter.

"I'm sure you've heard about the recent disappearance," Officer Moustache says.

Nia scoots her bike forward. "Yeah, about that, do you—"

Lyric grabs her arm and squeezes. She falls silent. *No police,* he silently reminds her with a stern look. She sheepishly nods.

"This is serious business." Officer Moustache leans out his car window. "We don't need you kids running around here. Y'all should stay close to *your* homes, stay out of trouble."

A muscle clenches so tight in Lyric's jaw, I'm worried it might snap. And Quincy looks like he's ready to bolt.

"Ya hear?" Officer Moustache says.

"Yep. Yes, sir. We totally heard every word," says Nia with a fake toothy smile.

"Good." Turning forward in his seat, he tugs his sunglasses down to the bridge of his wide nose. He shifts the car into gear and cruises down the street. Once he turns the corner, my shoulders slump in relief.

"Did we just get pulled over on our bikes for no good reason?" Nia asks.

"Guess we look suspicious," I say. Officer Moustache is gone but his warning lingers like a dark cloud.

"Told you! They only see what they want to. If Zee *could* explain himself, the cops would never believe him anyway. We can't depend on the police. We can only depend on each other. Kids helping kids." Lyric pedals angrily down the street, blowing past us.

We have to work hard to catch up with him. Quincy unsteadily follows as we ride past a brick sign with a plaque that reads "Meade Circle." The houses are nicer than in our neighborhood—all two stories with chimneys, garages, and tree houses. The lawns are green and cut low—no graveled driveways or concrete steps.

2302 Meade Circle. We brake at the end of the long driveway. Quincy slides off his bike, hitting the ground with a thud. "Need. A. Minute. I'll meet y'all up there," he says, panting.

Lyric, Nia, and I park our bikes near the mailbox. Rodrigo's house is brick with tall windows. A garden of colorful flowers surrounds the large porch. It's the kind of place you'd find in a magazine or on one of those fancy home-renovation shows.

I glance from Lyric to Nia. Neither one makes a move to approach the house. I step forward, my feet feeling like they're weighted with concrete. I'm halfway up the driveway and thinking about turning around when they join me.

I ring the doorbell. My hand shakes.

"I'll get it, Mom!" a boy calls out from inside.

The front door opens and a boy stands before us. His brown skin is lighter than mine and his eyes are so dark they appear to be black. He's about my height with hair gelled up in the front. He wears red-rimmed glasses that make him look cool and super smart.

"Rodrigo?" I ask.

"Yeah. Who are you?" He takes a step back and closes the door a little.

I point to myself. "I'm Justin. That's Nia and Lyric." I turn around. Quincy has made his way up to the porch. He still looks totally gassed. "And that's Quincy."

Rodrigo's dark eyes bounce to each of us. "What do you want?"

"We're friends of Zee," says Nia.

Apparently, that was the wrong thing to say. Rodrigo white-knuckles the doorknob. "I already talked to the police and that other guy. I—I got nothing else to say." He moves to shove the door closed.

Lyric surges forward and blocks it with his foot. "Wait. What other guy?"

"Let go or I'm gonna call my mom and dad!" Rodrigo pushes the door, but Lyric is stronger.

"Please. Just give us a few minutes," Nia begs, her hands folded under her chin. "Two other kids from our neighborhood are missing and we could be next."

Rodrigo squeezes his eyes shut. "No. Not again."

My mouth is so dry I have to swallow repeatedly to speak. "Not what again?"

His eyes flutter open and the fear reflected causes my chest to tighten. He peeks over his shoulder, then hesitantly steps outside onto the "Welcome Home" mat, closing the door behind him. "I—I thought it was over when Zee came back."

"What happened the day Zee disappeared?" Lyric asks. "You were the last one to see him, right?"

"They said I dreamed it. That I couldn't have seen what I saw." Rodrigo's body trembles along with his voice.

The hairs on my neck stand up.

"Dreamed what?" Quincy swats at a bug flying around his head, bobbing and weaving as the insect hovers.

Rodrigo's eyes glaze over. We wait and then wait some more. The world is silent around us. All of nature awaits his response.

Nia side-eyes me. Yeah, this is bad.

Lyric waves his hand in front of Rodrigo's face. "Hello?"

He jerks out of his daze, blinking hard. "Zee and I decided to sneak out of our cabin," he whispers. "He wanted to take some pictures, get some ideas for the art he was working on. We weren't going far."

"Camp. The woods. Getting late. Kids alone. That had bad idea written all over it," Nia mumbles.

"We lost track of time," Rodrigo says. His voice is hollow. It's almost as if he's talking only to himself. "It got dark and cold, but it had been ninety all day. Then the stars sorta, uh, flickered in and out like they were short-circuiting. And I thought . . ." He licks his lips. "I thought I heard something, a creepy voice, but maybe it was the wind. It was blowing hard."

Lyric, Nia, Quincy, and I exchange a terrified look. It wasn't the wind.

"We freaked and ran for camp. Zee was right behind me. He screamed. I turned around. I . . . I . . ." Rodrigo swallows loudly. "I could only see half of him, from the waist up. His legs were gone, like they had been sucked into a black hole."

Oh man!

Nia's hands fly up to cover her mouth, muffling her gasp.

Quincy sinks down on the steps and hugs his knees.

"It was like that magician trick where they saw someone in half. You know their legs are still there, but you can't see them," Rodrigo explains.

I shudder. No wonder Rodrigo is still shook and Zee is the way he is. How do you get past that?

Rodrigo extends his arm. "I grabbed Zee's hand. I pulled so hard, but whatever had him was much stronger. I couldn't see it, but it wouldn't let go. Zee was screaming, and I heard laughing." Rodrigo's voice cracks and his arm falls to his side. "Then he was gone. Like he was never there. Sometimes I still hear him begging for my help, but I couldn't do anything. It took him."

It! It! My skin crawls as I pace back and forth across the porch. "Oh man! I can't believe this."

"What?" Lyric asks.

I rub my palm down my sweaty face. "*It* took him? Like it could be a thing, not a person. A m-m-monster."

Quincy's head jerks back like I decked him.

"Duuuuudeee. Did you just go supernatural?" Lyric asks.

"I know it sounds crazy, but what else could have taken Zee like that?" My lungs constrict, filling up with water. I'm drowning. "Think about those spooky drawings on Zee's wall. And that mark is appearing out of nowhere. What else could do something like that?"

Lyric shoves both hands through his hair. "And our nightmares, the voices . . ."

"Monsters aren't real," cries Quincy. "They can't be."

Nia rubs her arms as if she's cold. "People always say that until they have a creepy encounter."

I look at Rodrigo. His face is a mask of terror and hopelessness. He wasn't kidnapped, but a part of him vanished that night at camp, too.

"What happened next?" Lyric asks, his voice faint.

Rodrigo lets out a shaky sigh. "I ran for help. I must have fallen and hit my head because I woke up and it was morning. Some of the counselors were standing over me. I told them what I saw, but no one believed me. They thought I was making it up so I wouldn't get into trouble for leaving camp." He smiles weakly. "I almost convinced myself Zee did run away. It was easier to believe."

Nia squeezes his shoulder and waits for him to look at her. "We believe you."

Rodrigo looks her directly in the eyes. "Something took Zee."

Quincy gulps loudly. "And it has my sister now. And Shae."

"Why did it go after Zee and not you? Is there anything else you can tell us?" I ask.

The front door flies open. A tall woman with long brown hair and a large mole on her cheek stands in the doorway. She frowns. "Estás bien?"

Rodrigo adjusts his glasses and stands up straighter. "Yeah. It's fine, Mom. I was just, uh, just talking to some friends from . . . the library."

The library? Her dark eyes are probing as they look us over. I'm not sure she believes him, but she says, "Your lunch is ready. You know how I hate for hot food to get cold. And we'll need to leave soon for your art and piano lessons."

"Okay. I'll be right in," Rodrigo says with a forced smile.

She hesitates, then walks back inside and closes the door.

Rodrigo's shoulders slump. "She'd be mad if she knew why you're really here. She doesn't like me talking about what happened at camp."

"Did you tell her the truth?" Nia asks.

He snorts out a humorless laugh. "Tried to. I learned fast to keep it to myself. I didn't wanna be *that* person—the strange kid who believes a monster kidnapped his friend by dragging him into a black hole. That kind of reputation would be impossible to shake."

"I'm sorry," says Nia.

"Look, I'm glad Zee's back and I'm sorry stuff is happening, but . . ." Rodrigo wrings his hands. "I can't—"

"Just a few more minutes, please," I say. "Did anything else strange happen that day?"

"Not that I remember," Rodrigo says. "We did normal camp stuff. There were different activities all day. Most of the time Zee did his thing and I did mine. He played games with some other kids, went swimming and stuff while I was hiking. We met up for dinner, then later . . . all that stuff happened like I said."

"What about a mark or bruise? Did you see one on Zee?" Nia asks.

Rodrigo's head tilts and his eyebrows crinkle as he thinks hard. "He had something on his wrist. He went to the nurse and she said it was just a bug bite."

"Uh-oh," Lyric says.

"Did it look like that?" I point to Quincy's arm.

Rodrigo backs away and covers his mouth like he's afraid Quincy is contagious. "E-e-exactly like that."

"No! No! It's gonna get me." Quincy roughly scrubs at the mark on his wrist. "I want it off! I want it off!"

Nia turns at me. "You were right. The mark means you're tagged. Are we all going to get one? Zee said 'one by one.' He drew a picture of everybody."

"Wow, just wow." Lyric falls back against the porch railing. "It really was a hit list. We're on a timer."

Rodrigo opens his door. "That's all I know. I—I gotta go." He hurriedly tries to enter his house.

My hand shoots out to block him. "Wait! One last thing. You said you talked to the police and another guy. Who did you mean?"

"Some ice cream guy came around here asking questions. I'd never seen him before. He had a long scar on his cheek," Rodrigo says.

"An ice cream guy with a scar?" Nia looks at me with wide eyes. "Could that be Hyde?"

My heart somersaults in my chest.

Rodrigo tries to close the front door.

"Sweet Dreams?" I ask. "Was it Sweet Dreams? This is important."

"Maybe! Now move. I don't wanna talk anymore!" Rodrigo says.

I release the door. It slams shut. Locks slide into place. Click. Click. Click. Three dead bolts just like Zee's room. The sound rings in my ears.

"Why would Hyde come here?" Nia asks.

My chest tightens. I tug the puzzle piece from my pocket and hold it tight.

"Justin?" Nia says.

"We should go." I need to move, to think. Rodrigo dropped several bombs on us and my mind is scrambled.

We hurry down the porch steps. At the end of the driveway we stop next to our bikes.

"Dude, what's going on?" Lyric grabs his head like it might

explode off his neck. "Hyde was acting strange yesterday, asking all those questions, but—"

"He brought that ice cream cart to Zee's welcome home party," says Nia. She has a tight grip on Quincy, who looks like a strong breeze might carry him away. "Why would he be after any of us?"

"Justin?" Lyric covers his mouth as if he's afraid of the words he's about to speak. "Shae was not Shae? What if Hyde is not Hyde? What if Hyde *is* the monster?"

I stare at him. So many thoughts swirl in my head, but I can't grasp just one. We could definitely be dealing with something supernatural and powerful. Quincy places his hand over the mark on his wrist. The waves of fear flowing off him are almost painful. He could disappear. So could Lyric. Nia.

I can't lose anyone else. Quincy jumps and spins around.

"What is it?" Lyric asks, on high alert.

Quincy swallows hard. "Uh . . . nothing. I thought I saw something."

"You okay?" Nia asks him.

He looks seriously creeped out. It does feel like we're being watched, but I don't see anything odd—houses, cars, trees . . . normal stuff.

Quincy rotates his shoulder; the motion causes the backpack to slip off his arms. It hits the ground.

"Hey, why don't you let me carry that for you?" Lyric reaches for the backpack, but Quincy quickly snatches it away.

"No. I got it," he says and tugs it back on.

Lyric side-eyes me. "No problem. Thought it looked heavy."

What's with Quincy and that backpack?

"Justin, what do we do now?" Nia asks.

The question echoes in my head. They watch me, their expressions a mixture of expectation and fear.

"Let's go." I pick up my bike and jump on.

"Where?" Lyric asks as they scramble for their bikes, too.

We need to figure this out. My eyes are focused on the road ahead. "To find Hyde."

09

We ride around town for almost two hours, hoping to spot Hyde's truck, but no luck. He wasn't at the Sweet Dreams shop. Nia tried searching for him on her phone, but couldn't find any information for "Hyde Miller." He could be anywhere.

"Stop. I need to stop," Quincy says, panting. He's slumped over his handlebars.

"I could take five, too." Lyric's face is red from the heat.

We're on the sidewalk in front of a small strip mall. It's packed with customers shopping at the food mart.

"I'm tired." Quincy collapses onto the ground. "We're never gonna find Hyde."

Nia sits on the curb and fans herself with her hand. We're all sweaty and smelly. "Maybe it's time to ask for some help."

"From who?" My skin is so hot it feels like it's on fire.

"I could call my mom and dad," Nia says. "Or maybe you can talk to Victoria. She's smart. She might—"

"We don't know anything. Nothing that's not . . ." I sigh. "Nothing that doesn't sound weird. Hyde is our one lead. He may have the answers, then we can ask for help."

Lyric nods. "Agree. We need to know more first."

"So, what now? We've been riding around forever. We don't know where Hyde is," Nia says.

I look longingly at the hole-in-the-wall bakery across the street. The sweet scent of freshly baked pastries drifts past me. My stomach growls, reminding me I never ate breakfast. Dropping that bowl of cereal in my kitchen this morning feels like forever ago.

"Should we split up?" I ask. "We'd—?"

"No way. In scary movies that never ends well," says Lyric.

"I don't want to be alone if . . . if . . ." Quincy says. His shoulders are slumped from the weight of the backpack. He rocks back and forth and hums to himself. The motion reminds me of Zee in his bedroom.

Nia gasps and points at Quincy.

He jumps. "What?"

"That tune you're humming . . ." she says. "I hear it, too. It sounds like—"

"The spooky ice cream music! It's from Hyde's truck." Guess my Dumbo ears are good for something.

Lyric's eyes widen. "Which direction?"

We all slowly spin around. The music grows louder.

"Eat ice cream and play. Eat ice cream and play. I scream, you scream. Eat ice cream and play." That strange jingle plays and repeats. Those high-pitched kid voices singing never stops being creepy.

"There!" Nia says.

Hyde's truck drives down the street, past the strip mall. He turns a corner.

"Let's go!" I jump on my bike as the others scramble to climb on theirs.

The chase is on. We dodge angry traffic as we race after the truck, weaving between cars. We cut across lawns and parking lots and swerve around buildings. Slow-moving pedestrians are not shy about voicing their annoyance.

My legs burn. I've never ridden this fast in my life. Wind whistles past me. My surroundings are a blur.

"Where is he going?" Nia shouts.

Hyde is heading out of town, the opposite direction of our neighborhood.

"We can't lose him," Lyric yells as he speeds up. I'm right there with him. Nia and Quincy are close behind. We continue our chase.

The music stops. Hyde turns left. Oh no. I recognize this area, this street. Hillcrest. My mom is buried at the cemetery on Hillcrest. Like this situation isn't messed up enough already.

My feet slip off my bike pedals and I swerve, almost crashing into Lyric before I regain my balance. I tighten my grip on the handlebars and concentrate on my breathing.

I haven't been to the cemetery since the funeral. My sister, Victoria, thinks visiting would be good for me. She's wrong. I said goodbye once, I don't want to do it every week or month. It shredded me to pieces the first time.

We race past Forest Hills Cemetery. It's a strange name because there are very few trees and the land is flat as a pancake.

Nia swings around me. Her bike is on my right, closer to the cemetery. Lyric positions his bike on my left. I'm boxed in. Protected.

I concentrate on pedaling down the too-quiet street. I will not remember burying my mom on a sunny, hot day in June. I will not remember that her grave is near a bench and cracked stone angel. I will not remember how nauseatingly sweet the flowers smelled near her coffin.

I will not remember that Mrs. Murphy stood beside me and held my hand as she cried. She loved my mom, but I think she was crying for Zee, too. Maybe she wondered if he was dead.

I will not remember thinking I might have to go to another funeral for Zee.

I will not remember walking away as they lowered the coffin and the feeling of my heart scattering in pieces across the ground.

I. Will. Not.

It's not until we clear the cemetery that I can breathe again. We ride two more blocks. Hyde's truck turns onto a private dirt road.

"Wait!" Lyric says.

We all skid to a stop. Black marks streak across the street.

"Why are we stopping?" I pant out.

Lyric wipes his hand over his sweaty, flushed face. "We need to recover and do a little surveillance. We have to figure out what we're walking into."

"Good idea." Nia slumps over her handlebars.

Quincy nods, too exhausted to speak.

We rest a few minutes then slowly pedal down the street. We stop near the driveway we saw Hyde enter: 307 Hillcrest.

It's a junkyard. We park our bikes on the sidewalk and stare at the large "NO TRESPASSING" and "KEEP OUT" signs on the chain-link fence surrounding the property.

"Uh, this is troubling," says Nia. "You think he lives here?"

"It's probably his evil lair where he hides the bad stuff he doesn't want anyone to find," Lyric says.

Nia and I share a look. Yeah, that's not the answer anyone wants to hear. Ever.

The front lawn, more weeds than grass, is covered with old appliances, dingy furniture, and broken electronics. Cars with corroded paint, shredded tires, and smashed headlights and windows form a hazardous maze.

"There's his truck." Lyric points to where it's parked at the end of the long driveway. It's next to a small green-and-white house. "Where did he—"

Hyde jumps out the side of his truck, carrying a box. A dog barks. The sound is loud and angry. This is not a small, friendly animal. From where we're standing, I can't see it. It must be behind the house.

Hyde walks in that direction, then pauses. "Again? I told you not to come back. You're wasting your time."

"Is he talking to the dog?" Maybe it's not his pet, but a stray or something.

"Go away." Hyde walks around the house, toward the backyard junk area. He whistles an off-key tune that makes me shiver.

Nia chews on her bottom lip. "I'm scared."

"Me too," says Quincy.

"Same," says Lyric. "But we came here to talk to him . . . find out what he knows."

"We can do this. We'll just ask him some questions and if we don't like his answers . . ." I swallow hard. "We'll get help."

"If we stick together, we'll be safe," Lyric says.

I nod and we walk up the driveway. With each step, I kick up a cloud of blood-red dirt that covers my white sneakers and the bottom of my jeans. Quincy, Lyric, and Nia follow closely behind me and I sense their anxiety—an additional heavy weight on my shoulders.

It suddenly hits me that this may be a very bad idea. Yeah, there's four of us and one of him, but we don't know what we're dealing with. We don't know how dangerous Hyde is.

"This place is spooky," says Nia as we approach the house.

The old wooden porch that wraps around the front is slightly tilted like a twisted smile. Two wide windows sit on either side of a black door. Eyes, nose, mouth. It's a creepy face. The house is alive, staring at me, smirking.

"Hyde?" I call out.

No response.

"Hyde?" My voice is louder this time.

No answer. I don't really want to stray too far from the house, especially since we heard a dog.

"Maybe he went inside through a back door," says Nia. "We should knock."

I climb up the porch steps and knock on the door. "Hyde?" I knock again. Nothing.

Lyric reaches around me and turns the doorknob.

"Don't—"

With a click, the door creaks open. I freeze, waiting for an alarm to sound or something scary to jump out and grab me.

"Man, why would it just open like that?" Lyric asks.

"We can't go in there. Close the door," Nia says.

A growl, deep and angry, rumbles through the air. I spin around and my stomach drops. A large pit bull prowls around the yard toward us. A spiked collar circles its thick neck and a leash trails across the ground. The flabby flesh around its mouth curls as globs of drool roll off its muzzle.

The dog eyes us like we're its next meal and it's starved.

10

"What are we gonna do?" Lyric whispers.

"I have some pepper spray on my key chain." Nia slowly reaches for her front pocket.

The dog snarls. Nia freezes.

"Don't move," I whisper.

With a whimper, Quincy dashes up the stairs. The pit bull leaps forward. Nia screams and leaps onto the porch. We race inside the house. I slam the door as the beast plows against it, barking and growling.

We're in Hyde's house.

"Dude—" Lyric says.

"Whatarewegonnado? Whatarewegonnado? Whatarewegonnado?" Nia walks around in a circle.

She's making me dizzy. Not the best feeling right now. I grab her by the shoulders and give her a little shake. "Nia. Stay with me."

"Okay, okay." She stares at me with wide eyes. "Searching for my happy, safe place." She blinks. Blinks again. "Still searching."

The pit bull growls and scratches at the door.

I release Nia and run a shaky hand over my face. Think. Think. Think. We gotta get out of here. My head whips around as I search—out of the corner of my eye, I spot something on the scratched-up hardwood floor.

It's a picture of Zee . . . his school photo. It's the same one they used on the news when he disappeared. Zee is wearing jeans and a white button-down shirt. He wanted to wear a superhero shirt for the picture, but Mrs. Murphy wouldn't let him.

I pick it up.

"Why does Hyde have that?" Nia asks.

"I don't know," I say.

She swallows hard. "Is this a clue? It proves something, right?"

The dog scratches at the door and whines. I flinch.

"Let's just leave. I wanna leave," Quincy says, clutching his backpack to his chest. "We can find Carla and Shae another way."

I hear a loud creak and spin around. Lyric is looking in a desk drawer he just opened.

"Hey, what are you doing?" I ask.

"We know something is up with Hyde. He rolled up on Rodrigo and asked all those questions. Now we find that picture of Zee . . . It's too suspicious." Lyric opens more drawers and rummages around.

"I thought the plan was to ask him some questions?" Nia tugs at her long braids.

"We might as well do a little investigating before he finds out we're here." Lyric peeks inside a large chest sitting next to the desk. "If we hurry we can be in and out before he knows anything."

I fold my hands behind my head and pace across the room. This is so messed up.

"Look for secret hiding places," says Lyric.

"Butch!" Hyde whistles loudly enough to be heard through the front door. "Come here, boy."

I hear the dog whimper, then the pounding of his paws as he runs across the porch toward the back of the house.

"Hurry!" says Lyric.

I leap into action. I run to a picture hanging crookedly on the wall. It's an old photo of a boy, possibly Hyde, when he was younger. His arm is around a small girl. There is a crack in the glass so I can't tell what she looks like. I peek behind the dusty frame. Nothing. I check a dirty floor vent. Nothing.

"This is so wrong, so wrong," Nia mutters. "We are gonna get in so much trouble."

She lifts cushions and runs her hands down the inside of the couch. She takes her hands out of the couch and shakes off clumps of brown pet hair and gray lint. "Yuck, yuck, yuck."

Quincy sticks his hand in a large vase, then checks a trash can. Empty. Lyric digs around in a potted plant. Just a dead fern. This is not going well.

I weave around the mismatched furniture and walk toward a tall bookshelf. Worn books are messily stacked on the shelves and look like they could topple at any moment. As I get closer, a cool breeze hits my face. The room is warm and I'm not near the window. That air has to be coming from somewhere.

I peer behind the bookshelf. Instead of a wall, I spot a door. "Uh, you guys. I think I found something."

They rush over.

"What is it?" Nia asks.

"There's a door back here."

"A hidden room! Dude, this is straight gangsta. Something important is definitely in there," says Lyric.

"Help me move it," I say. Nia and I shove one side, while Lyric and Quincy pull from the other end. Books rain down as the bookshelf screeches across the hardwood floor, revealing the door built into the wall.

"How do we get in?" I turn the knob. "It's locked. We need a key."

Lyric scoffs. "Please. Any kid with the right knowledge and"—he runs his hands through his hair and removes a small paperclip-like thing—"the right tools can pick this lock."

"Wow," says Quincy.

Nia's jaw drops. "Do you keep that in your hair?"

"My dad says you gotta be prepared at all times." Lyric gets to work.

Nia and I gawk at each other. Only Lyric.

Within seconds, Lyric has popped the lock. He moves to open the door and I grab his arm. "Wait." I lick my dry lips. "We don't know what's in there. What if—"

"We have to check it out," he says. "It might have the info we need to prove how scary and shady Hyde is."

"This could stop him from hurting any more kids and save us," says Nia.

"Okay, but we stick together." I release Lyric. He pushes open the door. The echoing screech as it scrapes across the floor sets off an attack of goose bumps.

A stale, musty smell rides the blast of cold air that whooshes out of the room. I stare into the dark space, and after a little nudge from Nia, ease forward. Quincy hovers in the doorway. One foot in the hidden room and the other in the living room.

I run my hand along the inside of the wall until I find a light switch. Electricity crackles through several bulbs hanging from the ceiling.

Nia and Lyric gasp. I hear Quincy gulp.

It's like we stepped into a police investigation room. One entire wall is covered with photos of kids. Names, ages, and dates are written under each picture; it reminds me of the family tree assignment I completed for my history class, only this is super disturbing.

I stumble closer on stiff legs. My eyes scan the faces. AnnaBelle Lee, age nine, disappeared from a school playground. Cameron Jones, age twelve, last seen at a zoo. Brian Kim, eight, went missing at a skateboard park. Tasha Wilkens, eleven, disappeared from a bowling alley. Oh man. Shae's up there, too.

"It's a freakin' missing wall," Lyric says.

"I think we found the evidence we need." I slowly spin around.

Another wall is a creepy art gallery of drawings, with squiggly lines and large splats of paint. It reminds me of the artwork in Zee's room—only bigger, messier, and scarier. There are images of hands clawing at headstones, a twisted tree with faces carved in the bark, a skeletal figure crouched down ready to pounce, and a dragon-like creature hovering in the air.

"Hey, does this mean Hyde's the kidnapper and monster? 'Cause I'm totally thinking this means he's our kidnapper and monster," Lyric says. "And we're in his house!"

It doesn't make sense. Was Zee warning us about Hyde? Why would he go after Carla and Shae? Why is he marking kids? *How* is he marking us?

Nia holds up several sheets of paper. Hyde has printed old missing-person articles. "There are pictures of other missing kids," Nia says. "Check out the dates. They disappeared over twenty years ago. Some have been gone even longer."

Lyric shoves his hands through his hair. "Do you think he's been kidnapping kids all that time? Wait, he couldn't have. They went missing before he was even born."

Quincy mutters to himself, rubbing his hands down his arms like he's cold. "This is a bad place. We shouldn't be here."

"What the—" Lyric holds up a yellow-stained sheet of paper.

"What is it?" Nia asks. We peer over his shoulder.

The ink is smudged, but I can still make out the headline on the article.

"Hyde Miller, age ten, disappears without a trace," reads Lyric.

"Like Shae and Carla," I say, my voice hushed.

"What else?" Nia asks.

Lyric scans the page. "He was found seven years later wandering near a lake. He was badly scarred and had amnesia. He couldn't tell anyone what happened."

My heart kicks my chest. This sounds eerily like what happened to Zee.

"Hyde disappeared and now he keeps track of missing kids," I say shakily. "Zee went missing. Shae is gone. Carla, too. Now Quincy is marked."

Nia grabs my arm. "What does this mean?"

"*That you're all next,*" a raspy voice says.

11

Lyric jerks, sending the paper flying up in the air.

I whip around so fast my spine cracks. "Who said that?"

The image on the wall shifts, paint swirling and melting down the wall. Red eyes appear and glow.

"I'll see you all. Soon," the voice says.

Nia screams. Or maybe that was me. We scramble over each other and race toward the door.

"Go, go, go!" I say. We spill into the living room.

Lyric shoves the door closed and backs away. "What was that?!"

"Was that Hyde? Where is he?" cries Quincy.

"Can't breathe." I lean forward, resting my hands on my knees. My heart is racing.

Nia tugs at my arm. "Justin. Was that the monster? It said it would see us soon."

My heart is pounding. I'm cold and hot and the combination makes me nauseous.

Lyric runs toward the front door and skids to a stop. He peeks out the window. "He's coming! Hyde's coming!"

"Oomph!" Lyric scurries back and slams into Nia.

Hyde is walking toward the house with the dog running by his legs. As Hyde grows closer, I hear his off-key whistling.

This is bad. Very, very bad.

He suddenly jerks to a stop and glances around. He's talking, but I'm not sure what he's saying. He looks annoyed.

"We have to go! Now!" Lyric says.

"Something's happening," cries Quincy, clutching his head. "I don't feel good."

We need another way out. I spin around, searching for a way to escape. I race into the adjacent kitchen, past a small dining area and into the laundry room. Over the washing machine there's a window facing the backyard. I unlock it and tug it open. "Hey, this way!"

The others hurry into the room as I peek outside and look around. Coast is clear.

"Nia." I help her climb out the window. She lands safely on the back porch. Quincy is next. Then Lyric.

The loud creak of the front door opening chills my blood. The dog barks and I hear its paws pounding in my direction.

"What is it, Butch?" Hyde asks.

I dive out the window, hit the porch with a thud.

The air crackles around me and my skin tingles. We leap off the steps and zip across the backyard. If we can make it to the street without being seen, we should be safe.

Our feet kick up dirt as we sprint around an obstacle course of rusty appliances.

"Quincy, hurry," Nia cries.

I spin around. Quincy struggles to keep up. With bulging eyes, he pumps his arms faster, but doesn't seem to pick up any speed. In fact, it looks like he's slowing down. He stumbles forward, falling to his knees. "Don't leave me!"

I start back toward him, but skid to a halt. "What—?"

An ink stain of darkness spreads across the sky. The turbulent breeze whips my clothes against my body.

A funnel cloud of dust spirals up out of the ground and attacks Quincy. "Ahhhhhh," he cries, caged within a dirt tornado.

I shield my face as swirling dirt stings my eyes.

Lyric staggers back from the force of the wind. "What's happening?"

A thunderous boom rips through the air. Lightning zigzags down from the sky, striking a pile of wood near Hyde's house.

Flames shoot up into the sky. Another bolt hits an overturned refrigerator. It explodes. Sparks fly.

The hair on my arms stands up and my body buzzes with energy.

"Stay away from all the metal!" Nia says. "It can act as a conductor."

"We're in a junkyard. There's metal everywhere," Lyric cries over the roaring wind.

"Justin!" The ground splits and a gaping hole forms around Quincy. He sinks, his legs disappearing into the earth. "Help!"

I dive for him and grab his wrists. He's waist-deep now and stares at me with wide, terrified eyes. "Hold on." He slides lower, pulling me forward on my stomach. The mark swirls and glows on his arm.

Suddenly, I'm jerked back. I look over my shoulder to see Nia holding my legs. Lyric clutches her ankles. We're a human chain.

Quincy's short nails claw down my arms until damp palms clamp my wrists. My limbs feel as if they're being torn out of their sockets. "Quincy, don't let go!"

Tears streak down his dirty face. "Justin." His clammy fingers slip through mine.

"No!" I scream, lunging for him. My fingers grab the fabric of his backpack. I rip off a pocket. He disappears, swallowed up as the ground closes over his head.

With a loud snap, the darkness recedes, creeping back until the sky is cloudless blue again. No more thunder and lightning. The brutal wind settles, replaced by a teasing, soft breeze.

I scramble back, slamming into Nia and Lyric. "What just happened? What just happened?"

Nia's arms wrap around me so tight it hurts. "It took him! Quincy is gone!"

Lyric jumps to his feet and clutches his head. "How is this possible? What are we gonna do?"

I push Nia's arms away and struggle to my feet. My legs give out and I fall to my knees doubled over. Need air. Sweat pours down my face, blinding me. My eyes sting as I shove my hand in my pocket and clutch the puzzle piece. I squeeze it until it folds. Breathe. Breathe. Sharp, hot pains shoot through my chest.

Nia lets out a painful cry. I turn to her as she extends her dirty arm. The swirl pattern appears on her wrist. Her skin blisters, forming the raised mark. I crawl closer. Lyric drops to his knees beside us.

"No," I whisper. My hand shakes as I reach for her. "No."

"One by one you'll disappear," Lyric whispers. Wide-eyed, he looks from me to Nia.

"It steals your soul," a deep voice says.

Ice forms in my veins. Booted feet step into my line of sight. My gaze travels up, past worn jeans and a black turtleneck. Hyde's scar ripples across his check.

"And eats your fear," he says with a wicked smile.

12

I scramble to my feet and jump in front of Lyric and Nia. "Stay away from us!"

The pit bull growls and crouches down as if it's ready to attack.

"Easy, Butch." Hyde tugs on its leash. "They've had a scare. They're emotional."

Lyric springs up, hands curled into fists at his sides. "Emotional! Emotional! Our friend just got swallowed up in the ground and you're . . . you're . . ."

Hyde crosses his arms and tilts his head to the side. "I'm what?"

Lyric falls silent and looks desperately at me. I reach behind me and help Nia to her feet. "We're leaving. Don't try to stop us."

"You're on private property. I can do whatever I want." Hyde scratches the side of his head as if he's thinking. "Like make you disappear, but I'll leave that to the Seeker. It has dibs." Hyde walks toward his house with a bounce in his step. Butch trots along beside him.

Seeker?

"What's he doing?" Nia asks. "He's just gonna let us leave?"

"Zee mentioned a Seeker," I say faintly. "In one of his creepy rhymes."

I stare into Nia's dazed eyes, then glance at her wrist. She's tagged now. I can't let her get taken. I have to save her.

"Wait!" I yell to Hyde.

He stops and peeks over his shoulder.

"Wh-what's a Seeker? Is that the monster?" I ask.

"Are *you* the monster?" Lyric asks, his jaw clenched tight. "Did you take our friends?"

I take a tentative step toward Hyde. "We came here for answers." My voice cracks. I tighten my grip on Nia's hand.

Hyde turns around and walks way. "Go away. Stop haunting me."

Confused, I glance at Lyric. He shrugs.

I trail Hyde across the backyard, ignoring the warning growls from Butch. Lyric and Nia are with me every step of the way. I need them close.

Hyde shakes his head and turns toward us. "You're wasting your time. I can't help you."

"Can't or won't?" Nia asks.

Hyde shrugs. "Both."

The glee in his voice makes me grind my teeth. Hyde climbs up his front porch steps.

Lyric shoves past me. "Hey! You think this is funny?! What's wrong with you?"

I try to hold him back. "Lyric . . ." He's shaking with rage. He jerks away from me.

Hyde spins on his heels to look down at us. "What's wrong with me?" He points to the scar on his face, then yanks off his leather glove.

Nia gasps and covers her mouth.

The skin on Hyde's hand is burned and mangled, with deep crisscross scars up to his arm. On his wrist, there's a swirl mark. I gasp. He's tagged, too.

"Do I care what's happening to you? No, because it won't fix this. Or make her go away," Hyde says.

Her? Who, Nia? It's like he's talking about someone not even here.

His wild, cold eyes scan our faces. This is what someone without a soul looks like.

"You can leave now. And don't come back." He shoves his glove back on.

No way! I run up the stairs, dodging the pit bull, and plant myself in front of the door.

"We're not going anywhere. Not until we get answers."

Hyde takes a threatening step toward me. The pit bull lunges. I sidestep it and narrowly avoid getting bit. Hyde tugs on the leash to hold it back.

"Hey!" Nia pulls out her phone. "Smile." She clicks a picture and types something quickly. "I'm recording. Make another move and I'm gonna put you on blast all over the internet. This will be viral in seconds." Her hand shakes. "This is Hyde Miller, y'all. If anything happens to us, he lives at—"

"Put that away!" Hyde yells and steps toward her.

Lyric slides in front of Nia with his fists raised. "Back up and call off your demon dog."

Hyde's jaw clenches. "Butch, sit."

With a growly whimper, the pit bull plops down, resting its large head on his paws.

Now what? It's a stare off. I have so many questions, I don't even know where to begin, so I spew everything in my head. "What's the Seeker? Is it a monster? What just happened to Quincy? Where is he? And Carla and Shae? Why do you have a mark? Why did our friends get marked? What does this have to do with Zee? How are you involved? Why do you have that missing wall? Why were you missing for seven years? How do we save Nia? Are we all going to disappear? How will the monster take us?"

Panting, I fall silent. We can start with those, but I have a ton more.

"Dude, you said all that without breathing," Lyric mutters. "That was cool, teach me later."

Hyde moves so quickly, I stumble back. Lyric catches me before I fall off the steps and hit the ground. With a smirk, Hyde sits on a porch chair.

"If you don't start talking right now . . ." Lyric nods at Nia. She holds the phone higher.

"You're being hunted," he says.

I gulp. Yeah, we kinda figured that, but to have it confirmed out loud is way different.

"By who?" My voice shakes.

"*You?*" Nia asks Hyde as she lowers her phone. On the screen I can see that she's still recording. Good.

Hyde hesitates, then says, "The Seeker. It's part of every game of Hide and Seek. If you disrespect its game in any way, it comes for you," Hyde says. "It *owns* you."

We gawk at him. Say what, now?

"Wait, wait, wait." Lyric holds up his hands. "You lost me at the Seeker. What or who is that?"

"It's . . ." Hyde runs a hand over his face. "It's hard to explain."

"Dude, figure it out," says Lyric. "What you're saying sounds not real, not possible. And if you're foolin' with us . . ." He gestures toward Nia's phone again.

Hyde's jaw clenches. The scar ripples down his cheek. "Look, I don't know exactly where it came from or how long it's been around, but it's really, really old. And it's connected to Hide and Seek." Hyde presses the heel of his palm against his forehead. "The game and the Seeker are one."

With a frustrated groan, I walk away a short distance. My linked hands rest on top of my head as I try to keep it from exploding. Hyde is lying. He has to be, but who would make up something like this?

I spin back around. "But *what is it*? What is the Seeker?!"

"I told you, I can't describe it," Hyde yells back. "A monster, an evil force . . . It doesn't matter. All you need to know is that it's coming for all of you!"

His words reverberate through my body. I draw in a loud breath as I stare at him. So many emotions flash across his face, but it's his haunted eyes that make my legs shake.

Nia places her hand on my shoulder and squeezes. "Breathe."

I didn't realize I wasn't. I exhale and inhale several times.

"A monster," Lyric mutters. That concept seems to be easier for him to handle. "And you're saying this thing is after us because of a stupid game?"

"Yeah." Hyde settles back in his chair. "You broke the rules."

"We did break the rules . . ." Nia says, as if she's talking to herself. Her eyes are distant. "No revealing the hiding place of a player. Carla did that with Shae. No hiding inside. That was Quincy." Her nose scrunches up, then she gasps. Her hand flies up to cover her mouth. "I—I blocked Quincy's path to the tree."

Lyric groans. "I kinda roughed up Quincy."

"And we never finished the game," I say. "We *all* broke the rules."

"One game. Five friends from the same neighborhood." Hyde rubs his chin. "That's never happened before."

"I just realized something." I glance at Nia and Lyric. "The marks are appearing in the order we broke the rules. Carla. Quincy. Nia . . ." My eyes widen.

"You get your mark when you're the next to go." Lyric's tortured eyes land on Nia.

Tears fill her eyes. She covers the mark on her arm.

No! I can't let this thing take her. I spin around to face Hyde. "What can we do? We made a mistake. How can we fix this?"

Hyde flexes his gloved hand. "Ever think you were meant for more, deserved more?" The corners of his lips lift into a sad smile. He stares back across the porch. I follow his gaze. There's nothing there.

"What is he talking about?" Nia asks.

He reminds me of Zee—lost and confused.

"Dude, what does this have to do with the Seeker and us?" Lyric asks.

Hyde blinks. His dark eyes clear. "In Nowhere—"

"What's that?" I'm so confused. He's talking in code like Zee.

"The place where the Seeker takes kids. The place where you're going." Hyde scoots back in the chair and folds one leg under the other. "The world . . . it's a game, too. A dark, twisted game you can't win. It's you against fear—yours and others. You run and hide, and sometimes you think you've escaped, but they always find you. It's the Seeker's rules. And it changes them so you never feel safe. There's only fear, fear, fear," he says in a singsongy voice.

I slump against the porch railing. How can any of this be real?

Nia's lips tremble. "How do we stop the Seeker?"

"You don't. You can't," Hyde says.

She wipes away a tear with the back of her hand. "I don't accept that. There has to be something we can do."

"This thing kidnapped you," I say. "How did you escape?"

Hyde touches his wrist, where his glove covers his mark. "I didn't."

Butch throws back his head and howls. I shudder.

"What do you mean?" I ask, unknowingly taking a step back.

Hyde leans forward. "The Seeker let me go so I could hunt kids, too."

13

Lyric's head jerks back. "You . . . you . . ."

"I made a deal to work for the Seeker."

He says it calmly, like he hasn't gut punched us.

"We should go." Nia tugs me by the arm. "I want to go."

We can't. We need more answers. "What does that mean, you work for the Seeker?" I ask.

Hyde hesitates and his eyes scan over us. It's clear he's choosing his words carefully—slowly luring us in.

"The Seeker needed help with his game. Needed more kids to play, possibly break rules. It offered me a deal. If I helped, I could come home."

"So, you're a traitor?" Lyric spits out.

"If that's the way you want to think about it," says Hyde with a dismissive wave of his hand.

"That's literally the only way to think about it," yells Nia.

"You don't understand what it's like there!" says Hyde. "I would have done anything to leave. If given the choice, you will, too."

Lyric shakes his head. "No, dude. We'd never betray each other or another kid. That's not how we roll."

Hyde laughs. It's sad. "Just wait until you're there a year, two, three, four." He gestures at his face and holds up his gloved hand. "When you're not fast enough to outrun your fears. When there's nowhere to hide."

"We won't be there that long," Lyric says.

"She thought that, too. They all think that." Hyde glances away.

I throw up my hands. I don't understand who he's talking about. "Who is *she*?"

Hyde runs a gloved finger down his scar. "No one."

Nia crosses her arms. "Zee escaped."

"Did he?" Hyde says quietly.

"What does that mean?" I ask.

"Just a question," he says cryptically.

"Why did you deliver that ice cream for Zee's party?" Lyric asks.

Hyde shrugs. "Because his mom called our store and requested a cart. We cater lots of kid events."

Nia gasps so loudly I jump. Her hand flies up to cover her mouth.

"What?" I ask.

She stares at Hyde with wide eyes, then slowly lowers her hand. "He works for the Seeker. Remember those ice cream wrappers. They were all about Hide and Seek."

It takes a moment before I get what she's saying. My jaw drops.

"It was all a setup?" Lyric cries. "You deliver ice cream with all kinds of info about the game, hoping, like, what? We play the game and do something to get taken by the Seeker?"

Hyde doesn't respond. He doesn't have to.

I swallow the sour taste in my mouth. "We talked about the game, and Shae arrived and wanted to play . . ."

Nia tugs at the end of her long braids. "But *how* was it Shae? She was supposedly miles away and wasn't even invited to the party."

Hyde jumps to his feet, startling Butch. "What did you say? What about Shae?"

"You have her picture up on your creepy wall, so you know she's missing," I say. "She supposedly disappeared from Lake Winnepesaukah campgrounds, but she was at Zee's party."

All the color drains from Hyde's face. He staggers back, falling against the side of the house. "Oh no."

Nia, Lyric, and I exchange a glance. What now?

"The Seeker . . . It must have been the Seeker." Hyde's eyes flutter closed and he trembles. "I didn't know it planned to—"

"Wait, you're saying the monster was pretending to be Shae?" Lyric asks. "It can do that?"

Hyde's eyes fly open. They're bright with terror. "As far as I know it's never physically left Nowhere. It needed help to capture more kids, that's why it sent me. It feeds off the fear of the kids in Nowhere and it's all about increasing the numbers. Its power is growing, but I didn't think . . ."

"Isn't that what you want? You work for it," I spit out.

Hyde shakes his head. "You don't understand! What if it decides that I'm failing? That I'm not completing my mission?"

"That's what you're worried about?" Lyric asks with disgust.

Hyde clutches his head with both hands. "What am I gonna do? I can't go back there."

I gawk. The selfishness oozing out of him makes me nauseous. He doesn't care about the kids he helped kidnap or us. It's all about him. "You don't want to go back, but it's okay we're being dragged there?!"

"Leave. Now! I don't care what you do with that video," he yells. "It won't matter anyway."

"You have to help us," Lyric says. "Tell us about Nowhere. How can we defeat this monster?"

We can't leave with nothing. No plan, no way to help Nia, to help *everyone.*

"Please." I'm willing to beg. "There has to be something we can do."

Hyde hurries across the porch toward the front door. Butch jumps up and trots after him, his leash trailing behind him. "Haven't you been listening? There's no way to stop it. The only way out is to work for the Seeker, and even then you suffer."

"What does that mean?" I ask.

Hyde hesitates, his hand on the doorknob.

"Please!" I cry again.

He flinches. After a long moment, his shoulders slump and he spins around. "You don't age in Nowhere. When the Seeker released me, I didn't know . . . Everything suddenly changes. The world was new, different. *I* was different. A teenager, but still a kid inside. A kid who'd spent years in a very bad place."

"I don't understand," Lyric says.

"I was ten when I was taken. I was there for seven years and didn't age, but the moment I returned I was instantly seventeen." Hyde visibly swallows. I see the ghosts of what he's experienced in his eyes. "Some of the kids in Nowhere have been there a very, very long time."

"Wh-what?" Nia asks, her voice shaky.

It's too horrible to comprehend.

I see the moment it truly hits Lyric. His jaw drops and his eyes grow as big as baseballs. "We could die. If we're there too long we could come back and die."

Hyde is lost in his thoughts. "All that time gone. I came back alone and my dad never forgave me. She never forgave me," he mumbles.

Nonsense. He's talking nonsense.

"There has to be a way to defeat the Seeker," I say.

Hyde shakes his head. "There's not. It *is* Hide and Seek. That's all it does. It has one mission, one goal to fulfill, and it won't stop until it does."

"What does that mean?!" Nia cries.

"You've got to help us stop this thing. You owe it to all the kids you helped kidnap."

I grab his arm and he jerks away so violently he stumbles back and almost falls.

"Don't touch me! Never touch."

"Sorry." I hold up my hands as if surrendering. "Sorry."

Tears fill his haunted eyes and for a brief moment I see that scared ten-year-old kid. He blinks and cold, calculating Hyde returns.

"You're on your own." He stomps inside the house with Butch and slams the door.

14

Lyric leaps onto the porch and bangs on the door. "Hyde! Hyde!"

I sink down on the steps and bury my head in my hands. Nia sits next to me.

"Open up! You have to talk to us," Lyric says.

From inside the house, Butch barks and growls. That's the only response we get.

"Lyric, stop." I turn to look at him. "He's not going to help." The weight of everything that has happened presses me down. The adrenaline seeps out, leaving me an empty shell. So tired—mentally and physically.

"He can't do this," says Lyric. "Nia, post that video. If the news shows up, I bet he'll start talking again."

"It won't stop what's happening," she says with a heavy sigh.

"Yeah, but . . ." Lyric swallows hard. "We can't . . . You heard what he said about that place. That thing is gonna take us. What if we're separated? What if we can't find each other?"

We fall silent. The shock of what we've learned doesn't wear off; instead it burrows deep, infecting us like an incurable virus. How do we recover from this? How do we survive?

"Even though we're down one member, we're still the Fantastic Four," Nia says.

Her eyes are bright with fear, but there's also something else. Determination. "The monster won't give up, but neither will we." She looks from me to Lyric. "Did you know everyone is born with the capacity to be brave? The key is to prepare yourself before the challenging situation."

I want to curl up somewhere and hide, but she's so Nia right now I can't help but smile.

"We can figure this out, right?" she asks.

She needs me to be strong. I can do that for her. I climb to my feet and extend my fist. "Together. Yeah, we can."

Lyric glances at Hyde's front door, then walks down the steps. He touches his fist with ours. "Count me in. I'm down for some monster butt-kicking."

This moment feels wrong, but also right. For now, I have Lyric and Nia, and I *almost* believe we can figure out a way to defeat the Seeker and survive. And maybe "almost" is enough.

I peek over my shoulder and see the blinds on a window flip closed. He'll never escape what he's done. He'll never be free of his guilt. It'll haunt him forever. What I saw in Zee, I see in him. But I want to help Zee. I believe there's hope for Zee. There's none for Hyde.

"We're kinda on the clock," Lyric says as we walk down the driveway. "So, what's the plan?"

I stare at Quincy's bike. He's gone. The panic I've fought back claws up to the surface.

"We need to break down everything Hyde told us. Everything we heard from Zee and Rodrigo, too." We pedal away from Hyde's place.

The wind whistles past me. We're traveling fast, but there's no outrunning this doom I sense closing in.

"Let's recap what we know," says Nia. We whip around a corner and swerve past some parked cars. "There's a Hide and Seek monster hunting kids who break the rules."

"Which we all did," interjects Lyric. He rides standing. His hair blows back off his face.

"It marks us before we're kidnapped and tormented with our worst fears," I say.

"And there's no way to stop the monster, so we need to figure out how to defeat it in Nowhere," Nia says.

We ride awhile in silence. Each of us lost in our thoughts.

"The backpack!" Nia yells suddenly.

She startles me and I fight to keep my balance on the bike. A car honks as I stray too far into the street. We cut across a park as we head toward our neighborhood.

"What are you talking about?" asks Lyric.

"When Quincy disappeared, he was wearing his backpack. It went with him," says Nia.

My eyes dart to her then back to the path. "That means there's a chance we can sneak stuff inside with us. Stuff that could help us defeat the monster!"

"That's genius," says Lyric.

"Whoa!"

I glance over at Nia. She wobbles on her bike. The pedals spin at a blinding rate. Her legs are outstretched to avoid being cut. "What's happening?!" She zooms forward, swerving around bushes and trees.

"Nia!" Lyric and I race to catch up with her.

The bike tilts. She tumbles off into a thick patch of grass. I jump off my bike and run over to where she lies. "Are you okay?" I reach for her hand and my fingers pass through her. She's blurry, ghostlike.

I gasp. "No."

Lyric runs up beside me. He attempts to pick her up, but only grabs air. "What—?"

"The Seeker," I whisper.

"Justin?" Nia stretches her arm out toward me.

I extend my trembling arm. My fingers tingle as they sweep through her rippling image. Not yet! I'm not ready.

Lyric runs one way, then darts back. "We need help! Help!"

There's nothing we can do, nothing anyone can do. My heavy arms drop to my side.

Nia starts to fade. Tears trail down her cheeks and her chin trembles. "Find me."

I nod and blink my blurry eyes. "I p-promise."

Behind Nia, a large shadow creeps across the grass. A deep, growly voice says, *"One by one you'll disappear. I steal your souls and consume your fear."*

Lyric cries out. He staggers back, loses his balance, and falls to the ground.

The shadow slowly morphs into that grotesque drawing from Zee's wall. Different body parts appear—the insect-like legs, the scaly thin arms, the claws, the wings with spikes, the oversized head with the red eyes. One by one they connect, until the horrifying creature stands before us.

I'm frozen in place.

The Seeker reaches for Nia. She's a blurry version of herself. Transparent. I can see right through her.

One claw hand tugs Nia into its body. The Seeker's black wings wrap around her, hiding her from my view. *"And then there were only two,"* it growls.

Nia screams. She and the Seeker disappear.

Terror and pain rip through me. My legs buckle. "Noooooo!"

15

My knees hit the ground hard and I fall forward, bracing myself on my hands. There's pain all over my body, but it's strongest around my heart. Nia is gone.

I grab my chest, my hands twitching. Nia needs me. I promised I'd find her. I can't let my promise turn into a lie. Breathe! Inhale. Exhale.

"Justin?!"

Lyric's voice sounds like it's underwater. My vision fades in and out. I'm on fire and freezing at the same time—sweating and numb.

Panic attack. A bad one.

Nia.

Quincy. Carla. Shae.

Zee.

Mom.

Everybody leaves. I can't stop it. Sweat trickles down into my eyes, mixing with the tears already there.

Soul hurts.

"Justin! I got you." Lyric crawls over to me.

I struggle to lift my heavy head. He's pale, and his eyes are bright with tears. "Nia." My voice is so hoarse, I don't sound like myself.

"I know, man. She . . ." He wipes his eyes with the back of his hand. "She's gone."

I flinch. The words sting.

My muscles are wet noodles. I flop around before steadying myself, turning so I'm sitting on my butt. I wrap my trembling arms around my bent legs and rest my head on my knees. One. Two. Three. Four. I count my breaths as the python slowly loosens its hold around my heart.

"It's going to be okay," Lyric says.

I would scoff but I don't have the energy. How is anything okay? Look at me. What if I have a panic attack when we get to Nowhere, when we're fighting the Seeker? No one should depend on me. *I* can't depend on me. If we fail, it'll be all my fault.

I tilt to the side, lifting my butt so I can reach the puzzle piece in my back pocket. My fingers clench it tightly; the cardboard bites into my palm. It only calms me a little.

Minutes ticktock by. As I inhale and exhale, air begins to smoothly circulate through my lungs. My eyes cross as I stare at the cracks in the speckled concrete. Red ants play peekaboo, crawling in and out of the gaps.

A lawn mower sputters to life in the distance. Birds tweet, annoyingly, above. The buzz of voices and laughter from nearby houses taunt me. Children laugh as they run around the park. The world goes on like nothing's happened, just like after my mom died. It's not fair.

"I bet when you woke up this morning, this isn't how you thought the day would go down, huh?" he says. "Me either. I keep thinking, if I were a superhero, what would I do right now?"

I slowly lift my head and turn to Lyric. He's staring off in the distance. He looks tired, but somehow calm despite everything that has happened.

He faces me. "We're gonna get her back, everybody else, too."

I snort out a laugh. "What's wrong with you? Have we been living the same day? All we've done is lose. And now with Nia . . ." I swallow hard. "How are you holding it together?"

He tugs at the rip in his jeans near his knee. "I'm not gonna lie. I'm freaked out, like mentally in a corner rocking back and forth and crying right now."

Okay, that's something, I guess.

His shoulders slump. "It's just . . . with everything that happened with my dad, I've learned that bad stuff happens all the time.

Sometimes you cause it, sometimes it just happens." He shoves a hand through his hair. "You kinda have to roll with it and trust in the people close to you to have your back. We're in this together. We'll figure it out."

"How can you be sure?"

"Fixing stuff and helping people is your thing," he says with an easy shrug.

"Uh, no, it's not." What is he talking about?

"In third grade, who took down that kid who stuffed Zee in a dumpster? Who made math study cards for Nia last year when she was worried she wouldn't pass?"

"Lyric, that stuff—"

"Who collects recycling and cuts grass to help Victoria pay the bills? Who put up flyers when Zee disappeared?"

"Stop."

"Who slept at the hospital with his mom when she was real bad? Who goes with me to visit my dad in jail? Not just once. Or twice."

"Lyric—"

"You've gone *every time*. Even after your mom died. You had other stuff to do, more important stuff. You didn't have to come with me, but you did!" He's yelling now and breathing hard.

My eyes sting. "You don't understand."

"You always find a way to make stuff better," he says as if he didn't hear me. "You're always there for me."

Anger whips through me. I surge to my feet. "You're wrong. Stop believin' in me."

Lyric gawks at me as he slowly stands. "Wow. Dude . . . Wow. That was stupidest demand in the history of demands." He shakes his head like he's disappointed. "I'm kinda embarrassed for you right now."

I wince.

"You don't want people to believe in you? Man, you're one of my best friends because *I can believe in you,* because I can trust you. All day, every day. You got me. And I got you." He crosses his arms. "You get a pass 'cause we're dealing with some seriously bad stuff, but don't *ever* say something stupid like that again."

I stare at him. He doesn't understand. I try to force words out to defend myself, but they won't climb out of my tight, dry throat.

He holds my gaze, not backing down. "Take the pass and let's move on. We got things to figure out before it's too late."

I exhale and release the pain from all my swirling emotions in one loud breath. "Sorry. It's just . . . Never mind." Lyric is right. I need to let it go for now. I gotta pull it together. Nia is depending on me.

"So, we good?" One blond eyebrow arches.

"Yeah. We're good." Not even close, but I gotta stop whining. I'm annoying myself.

"Cool." He extends his fist. I reach out to bump it with mine and spot the mark on his wrist. My eyes fly up to meet his.

"When?"

He avoids my eyes. "After Nia was taken."

"Why didn't you say anything?!"

"What's to say? We knew it was coming."

"I know, but . . ."

Lyric lightly punches me in the shoulder. "C'mon, dude. Let's not make this a moment."

He stares at me, his eyes pleading. He's holding it together, barely. A lot of people don't get to see the real Lyric. They buy into all the negative stuff they hear about his family and expect him to be a certain way, but he's so much more. He's loyal, generous, hilarious. He's not as hard as he pretends. He keeps things close and he doesn't trust everybody with his friendship and emotions. He trusts me.

I nod. "Yeah, okay."

He smiles. "About those backpacks . . . I think Nia is right and that could work. I'm sure I can find some supplies at home that may help. My dad has this secret storage closet . . ." He shakes his head like he's let something slip. "Forget I said that. Just know I got us covered."

"I'll pack stuff, too." We have no idea if this will actually work, but this is the only plan we have. And yeah, we may get things inside, but how do we defeat the Seeker? We know nothing about it.

"I see the wheels turning," Lyric says. "We're gonna figure it out. We don't know all the details about what's about to go down, but we're a team. We got this," he says, like it's the only option. "And when we get back, I'm gonna pay Hyde a little visit. He did us dirty and I can't let that slide."

Uh-oh. I don't want to know what he has in mind. Lyric is creative.

With a smirk, he backs away and salutes. "I'll see you on the other side."

"Wait. You're leaving?"

"Don't know how much time I have left. Got business to take care of," he says. "There's a lot of monster butt-kicking to prepare for."

"Yeah, okay." He's right. What did Nia say? To be brave you have to prepare before the challenging situation.

"What should we do with Nia's bike?" Lyric asks.

"I'll take it with me." We had to leave Quincy's. I won't leave hers.

We awkwardly stare at each other for a long moment.

He runs a hand through his hair. "When you get there, look for me, okay?"

"That's the first thing I'm gonna do. Find you and Nia. And nobody will be left behind. We're coming home together."

With a little chin lift, he grabs his bike and walks away, holding it by the handlebars. With his other hand, he reaches into his pocket and removes his harmonica, playing a hauntingly off-key song.

He walks toward the setting sun. The orange glow creates a halo effect around him as he disappears around the corner. My heart kicks, then settles after a few deep breaths. I will see him again. I have to.

I walk the bikes toward my house. My legs shake. I'm drained and each step takes a huge effort. The world around me is different now, shaded with dread. I don't even feel like myself anymore. It's like I'm missing already.

Victoria's green Honda is parked in the driveway. I'm both sad and happy she's home. I could tell her what's happening, but would she believe me? She couldn't stop it. She'd have to watch me leave like we watched Mom go. Maybe not knowing is better. Maybe I won't be gone long enough for her to miss me.

I park the bikes near the garage and stand in the driveway, not quite ready to go inside. The front door swings open and Victoria steps onto the porch. "Yes, you live here. You gonna stand there all day or what?" With arms crossed and head cocked to the side, she looks so much like Mom my heart hurts. She even wears crazy, bright colors head-to-toe like Mom—today is yellow. She looks like a giant banana.

I force a smile. "Ha, ha." I stroll up the steps. "Since it's your day to cook, I was tryin' to figure out if I should risk my life again. Last week you 'bout killed me with your tuna surprise. I guess the surprise was food poisoning."

"Shut up." She surges forward, wraps her arm around my sweaty neck, and drags me inside the house. I could totally break this chokehold 'cause I watch wrestling and know some slick moves, but I let her rough me up a bit for fun.

"Eww, you are so funky." She shoves me away and shudders, glancing down at her clothes. "Now I'm all gross."

"You're always gross," I say as she pushes me into the kitchen and down on a chair.

She swipes her curly black hair off her wide forehead and tries to glare at me, but her lips twitch. "Whatever, troll boy."

"And you're supposed to be the mature one." I roll my eyes.

She wets some paper towels and throws them at me. I wipe off my face and clean my hands. I covertly sniff my armpits and grimace. Got that outside smell—dirt, sweat, grass—with an added scent of fear.

"I know it's a little early for dinner, but I gotta meet my study group." Victoria gestures at the brown paper bags.

My stomach growls. "Takeout?" We don't have a lot of extra money since she's the only one working an actual job.

"Orange chicken and shrimp fried rice from Wok and Roll. Thought we deserved a treat." Nia hates take-out containers. She says they make the food toxic and everything ends up tasting like Styrofoam. It takes five hundred years to decompose, which is bad for the environment. *Nia.*

I rub my cold hands along my thighs as Victoria heaps food on my plate.

The phone in the living room rings.

"I'll get it," I say.

"No, don't worry about it. It's probably just a bill collector. They'll leave a message and call back like always."

My fork freezes halfway to my mouth. Should I tell her about the woman who stopped by yesterday from the utility company? Victoria is in a good mood and we haven't had dinner together in a long time. The bills aren't going anywhere and there's nothing we can do about it right now. And our problems are much bigger than a late notice.

The ringing stops. From the other room, I hear the click of the answering machine and a muffled voice leaving a long message.

"So, why are you so nasty? What've you been up to today?" She pours us some soda and sits across from me.

I stab a piece of chicken with my fork. "Uh, nothing much. Hanging out with Nia and Lyric," I mumble.

"Staying out of trouble?"

"Mmmm-hmmm." My throat burns.

"Hey, with that Shae Davidson girl missing and all, you should stay close to home until the police figure it out. Don't be roaming around, okay?"

"Yeah, uh, sure." I take a bite of orange chicken. Tastes like tangy dirt. Can't even enjoy my last meal.

When Mom was alive, the kitchen used to be my favorite place in the whole house. My friends would come over and hang out, and we'd play games and work on puzzles together.

Victoria tries hard to keep things normal for me with the family meals, helping me with my homework and stuff, but she gets busy with college and her jobs.

"Why are you looking at me like that?" she asks through a loud yawn.

The heavy bags under her brown eyes make them appear bigger. Is that a gray hair?

She sighs when I don't answer. "Justin?"

"I'm just wondering why you don't close your mouth when you eat." I fake shudder. "It's disgusting watching your food slosh around like that."

She growls and throws a fortune cookie at me. It bounces off my head and hits the floor. "Ouch. That's gonna leave a bruise."

"Shut up."

"That's the best comeback you got? What's up with you?" She's usually quick with the insults. As a big sister it's pretty much required.

"I'm being nice. You should try it."

My eyes narrow. "First takeout and now 'nice'? What's going on?"

The last time she acted this weird was when she told me about Mom's cancer. My stiff fingers curl around the seat of my chair. Oh no. She's been tired lately, lost a little weight. She cut her hair, but maybe it's falling out. Is she sick like Mom? My pulse rockets into space.

She eyes me uneasily. "I wanna talk to you about something."

"Wh-what?"

"I think we need a roommate," she blurts out.

Roommate? That's why she's acting strange? "You want someone to live with us?" I gulp down some soda. The liquid cools my overheating body and I slump against my chair in relief.

"With all these bills, we need the money. My friend Undrea—"

"If she's willing to sleep on the couch, I don't care." Seems like a bum deal to me and it sucks I won't be able to hang out in the living room and watch television, but I'll make it work. That's if I'm here anyway. If I don't make it back, at least Victoria won't be alone. I'd hate for her to be sad all the time.

Victoria stares at me for a long moment. "Undrea would take Mom's old room."

The fork slips from my fingers and hits the table with a clack. "Uh, no. Mom's room . . . No."

Victoria sighs. It's loud and long. "We've talked about cleaning out her stuff for a while now."

"No, we haven't. You talk and I refuse to listen. So technically—"

"It's time, Justin. Your counselor even believes if you accept she's not coming back your panic attacks might stop and—"

"First, I thought my conversations were private. Second, I'm much better." Lie, but whatever. She set me up with this dinner. The orange chicken and rice churn in my stomach.

"I'm trying to do what's best for us. Don't you want to stay here?"

How could she wanna get rid of Mom's stuff, forget about her?

"Okay, just calm down. Justin, breathe."

Didn't realize I wasn't. She's a little fuzzy so I blink hard. "I vote no on the roommate. I'll find more jobs. More recycling and cutting lawns. I'll do anything. We don't have to gut Mom's room."

"It's been over a year."

Three hundred and ninety-eight days.

"She's not coming back," Victoria says softly.

I grit my teeth so hard my jaw snaps. "I know that!"

"I'm sorry. It's just . . ." She blinks back tears and smiles weakly. "Think about it. We can talk later, okay?"

All kinds of thoughts and feelings bubble up inside me, but I swallow them down. This isn't how I wanted to spend my last moments with her.

She toys with her food. "So, you hate me now? I suck at being a big sister?"

My gaze drops to the table. The fire in my throat is only a little less intense than the blaze behind my eyes.

"Hey, you're supposed to disagree."

I shrug. "You do suck at it sometimes."

"I'll work harder at not being so annoyed by you," she says with a huff.

For a little while longer we can go on pretending everything's okay. "I'll work harder at not finding you so annoying."

She throws another fortune cookie at me, but I'm ready this

time. I catch it before it hits me in the head. Miss the other two, though. "Owww."

The clock in the living room chimes loudly. I jump. Time is speeding away and I have no idea when I'll be taken. The waiting and not knowing is another way the monster torments us.

Victoria stands. "I need to get to my study group."

"You're leaving? Already?"

She throws away her trash. "Open your fortune cookie."

My fingers fumble with the wrapper and break the cookie in half. "Your greatest danger comes from within."

Pfft. Danger within? I have panic attacks, but that's nothing compared to what I'm facing. The Seeker is coming for me, and it won't stop until I'm trapped in its world of horror. That's an *outside* danger. Bet no one would ever find a fortune like that in a cookie.

"My turn." Victoria breaks her cookie and removes the small slip of paper. "Your brother is a troll, but he will repay your kindness by cleaning up and doing his chores."

"Ha, ha, ha." The insults are back. This I can deal with. I launch a fortune cookie at her.

She ducks and runs toward the back door. "Love you, too. And try not to break any more dishes, will ya?"

"Huh?"

"Your cereal bowl. Pieces were all over the sink."

I wince. "Uh, sorry."

She picks up her purse. "Hey, we're good, right?"

"Vic, I . . ." The words get stuck in my throat.

"Yeah?"

A pain pierces my wrist. I flinch and glance down to see the mark blister my skin. Tagged. I'm next to go. That means Lyric must be gone.

I jump up. My chair tilts on the two back legs, then crashes to the floor.

"Justin?"

My breathing is choppy. I run to the kitchen sink and fight not to get sick. I grasp the edge of the counter. Inhale. Exhale. Inhale. Exhale. I'm the only one left.

Victoria walks up next to me. "You okay?" She places her hand on my forehead. I flinch from the coolness of her touch.

I want to say something, everything. I want to tell her that I'm glad she's my sister and I appreciate her though I don't show it enough. Tell her I'm scared almost all the time and that I hate she has to work so hard. Tell her that I have to go away and that she's one of the reasons I'm gonna fight hard to get back. Tell her Mom would be proud of her. I want to tell her goodbye.

I turn and force a smile. "I'm okay. Just ate too fast and felt a little sick."

She frowns. "You sure? You—"

"I'm good. Really."

She stares at me so intensely I squirm, but I hold her gaze. I don't want to worry her.

"Hey, how about next weekend we hit up the arcade? And maybe I can swing a movie."

Wow, she really feels bad for upsetting me. "You hate the arcade."

"Yeah, there's a lot of loud, stinky kids, but I do love beating you at that dart game," she says.

"That was once and only because I had the shakes from that supersized soda." I lift my hands high in the air. "I am dart champion of the world." I cheer for myself and bow.

She snorts. "Whatever. So we're on? Date night with your favorite sister?"

"You're my only sister and eww." I fake shudder. "Never mention 'date' and 'sister' in the same sentence again. You're on. Can't wait to take you down." I wiggle my big ears. "And *hear* you admit defeat."

She laughs, holding her stomach. I'll carry that sound with me.

"I won't be gone too long. Keep the doors locked, okay?"

"Yeah." That won't save me from the Seeker.

She hesitates with her hand on the doorknob. "I see you, Justin."

That's something Mom said. She thought people used "love" too carelessly. To "see" someone was understanding who they are deep inside—good, bad, and everything in between. Having a forever soul connection that lasted for eternity.

I clear my throat. "Bye, Vic."

She walks into the dark night. The door slams closed, the sound final. I fall back against the counter, as the last of my energy seeps from me. Pretending to be okay was hard, but I know not telling her was the right thing to do.

The kitchen is too quiet. What do I do now? I could be snatched at any moment. Will it hurt? How long will it take?

I mentally shake myself. Gotta stay focused and alert. I run down the hallway and into my bedroom to grab my backpack from the closet. I dump out the junk inside and rummage through drawers and closets for basic survival stuff to take—flashlight, rope, scissors, matches, hand wipes, first-aid kit. I bet Lyric has way cooler items to pack. I save a little room for food—packaged cookies, peanuts, and some water bottles. We have no idea what the food situation is like.

After tossing away my trash and washing the dishes I wander around the house with my backpack securely on my shoulders, trying not to think about the fact that I'm being hunted.

My feet are on autopilot and guide me to my mom's bedroom. Like it has a mind of its own, my hand reaches for the loose doorknob and turns. There's a click and the door drifts open. My heart skips a beat. I haven't been inside since she left.

The bed is neatly covered with a yellow floral comforter. Her slippers sit on the rug next to the nightstand. Pictures are scattered across the dresser. The television screen is covered with a thick layer of dust. Dozens of prescription bottles cover a small folding table near the window.

Sniffing the air, I search for my mom's sweet, fruity scent but only the fragrance of sickness remains. Now I understand why Victoria keeps the scarves in a Ziploc bag. It's to save Mom's smell for as long as possible.

Hovering in the doorway, I stare at the unfinished jigsaw puzzle on her desk. The missing piece burns a hole in my back pocket. "You were supposed to get better." My voice cracks. "You *promised* you wouldn't leave."

Promises are lies, easily broken. And I promised Nia . . . I stagger back and start to close the door when the television suddenly switches on. The sound of crackling static fills the room. The snowy, white brightness of the screen is blinding.

"I saved the best for last," a growly voice says.

"No!" A tingling sensation spreads from my toes, up my legs, throughout my entire body. My feet slide forward like I'm being drawn by a magnet.

I dig my sneakers into the carpet and thrust my body back, but a stronger force pulls me harder, controls my movement. My arms flail as I struggle to hold on to the furniture, to anything solid to stop my momentum. In the back of my mind I know it's useless, but I need to fight. Can't go down so easy.

Framed photos and a lamp crash to the floor as I sideswipe the nightstand. I desperately grab for the bed, ripping the comforter from the mattress. Yanked off my feet, I zoom toward the television and brace myself for impact. At this speed, the collision is gonna leave a big mess.

My hands fly up to protect my face, but instead of slamming into glass, cold air, thick and heavy, squeezes my body. I crack open my eyes as I'm sucked deeper into darkness.

I'm weightless, spinning violently. I plummet down like I'm on a mile-high roller coaster. Air whistles through my ears.

My head snaps back. I'm jerked upward, then slammed down. Everything goes dark.

16

My eyes fly open. The darkness is so thick it takes my breath away. What . . . what happened? Where am I? Suddenly, like water spewing from a faucet, memories flood my mind. The Seeker! It came for me!

I jerk up, smacking my head against something solid. “Owww.” The pain hits as a lump instantly forms on my forehead. It throbs to the frantic beat of my heart. I hold still and wait for the dizziness to pass. My back is slightly arched and as I wiggle around a little, I realize I’m lying on my bulky backpack. The straps are tight around my shoulders.

It made it to Nowhere with me.

Nia was right. There's no time to celebrate, though. I have to figure out where I am.

I inhale a deep breath. The air is humid and I smell . . . dirt. I slowly stretch out my trembling arms. I can't extend them fully because of whatever is above me. My fingers slide over something coarse, with a wavy pattern. Wood maybe?

My hands shake but I keep reaching out. To my left and right, more wood. Beneath me, wood. Wiggling around, I'm able to judge the size of the enclosure. It's small, just a little wider and longer than me. I'm trapped in a Justin-sized box?

A dark, wooden box the size of a person. It's a coffin! I'm buried alive!

"Noooooo! Help! Somebody help me!"

I push and kick at the wood, but I'm like a turtle on its back, flailing helplessly. "Help! Let me outta here!" Air. Is it running out? I'm gonna suffocate. Can't breathe. I'm dying. My body will shrivel, wither away until only dry bones are left.

"Help! Please!" I'm breathing so fast air whistles out of my nose. My stomach lurches, sending up partially digested orange chicken and fried rice. I slap my hand over my mouth and squeeze my eyes shut. I swallow back down the sour taste and struggle to control my breathing.

One . . . two . . . three . . . four . . . five. Inhale. Exhale. One . . . two . . . three . . . five . . . Inhale. Exhale. Breathe! Tears trickle out the corners of my eyes and I'm trembling so violently my teeth chatter.

Breathe. I'm alive. I'm not dying. I have plenty of air. The walls of this box are not closing in on me. I imagine wide-open spaces—acres of farmland, a desert with miles of rolling dunes, a football field, the large park near my house, empty beaches . . . Breathe. Count. Breathe. Count.

I clench my eyes closed and for some reason this darkness is not as scary. I'm aware of everything—the weight of the locs on my forehead, the sticky sweatiness of my body, the harsh sound of my breathing, the rough texture of my clothes against my cool skin.

"Justin." It's a faint whisper. So low, I think I imagined it.

"Who's . . . who's there?" My voice is weak.

There's no response. I wait. All my nerves are on edge. "Who's there?!"

I swallow hard. My nails claw into the wood beneath me as a swell of anger rolls through me in waves. The Seeker did this.

"I hate you! Do you hear me?! I hate you!" I kick the lid. It creaks but doesn't break.

The Seeker took Zee away from me. It broke him and I may never have my friend back. Mrs. Murphy went through so much while he was gone and she's still suffering. I needed my friend, especially when my mom died. And he wasn't there because of the Seeker.

It came for us—Shae, Carla, Quincy, Nia, and Lyric. It hunted us, tagged us, terrified us, and brought us to this horrible place. It has my friends. What's Nia going through right now? And Lyric?

Victoria . . . When she realizes I'm gone, she'll be hurting, too. She'll be alone.

I have to get back to my sister. I have to find everyone and get us all home. Sweat trickles down my face and into my eyes. It stings. I breathe through the pain, focus on it. It fuels my determination to escape and make the Seeker pay for all that it's done.

Every helpful tip my counselor has ever shared about dealing with stressful and scary situations comes back to me. This is the perfect time to put them all into practice. Breathe. Count. Focus. Release. Recover. I slide my hand into my pocket. The puzzle piece is there.

It feels like forever, but my pulse gradually slows until my heart is no longer battering my chest. "Think. There has to be a way out."

Wiggling around the cramped space, I push at the lid, straining until my arms tremble and fall limply to my side. I wait for the ache in my muscles to fade. I have to break through the wood. I grit my teeth and punch the lid. My knuckles scream in pain. The lid splinters.

I punch again. Again. Again. My hand throbs. With a cry of rage, I put all my fury behind one powerful swing. The crack widens. Cold air seeps through the opening. I wait for dirt to pour inside. Nothing. Maybe I'm not underground after all.

Bam! Bam! Bam! More hits and kicks. A larger gap appears. There's light. It's faint but I see it. An unhuman sound erupts from me as I pry the wood back, ignoring the pain in my palms. My arm shoots out of the open space, and then I manage to push my head and torso through.

Panting, I glance around to see that I'm in a large hole in the ground. It's a least six feet deep. *It is a grave,* only I haven't been buried . . . yet. Above me the sky is a gloomy gray. It weeps drops of freezing rain.

I hurriedly squeeze the rest of my body out of the coffin. Once I'm standing on top of it, I breathe a little easier. Now I gotta get out of this hole. I tighten the straps on my backpack, wincing from the pain throbbing in my bruised hands.

I press against the wall of dirt. It's solid enough for me to get a good hold. I dig my fingers deep inside, and like I'm rock climbing, I pull myself up. The soil stings the cuts on my hands. My arms shake from the effort to lift my weight. I grit my teeth and keep going.

With the last of my energy I lurch upward. My numb fingers dig into the ground outside the grave. I heave myself out and roll as far as my exhausted body will allow.

Panting, I collapse, my weary limbs tangled around me. I did it. I'm free. Wiping a hand down my face, to clear away the dirt and sweat, I glance around. My gaze lands on a tombstone, but it's not mine. It's my mom's.

Helen Vaughn. Beloved Mother and Wife.

17

With a whimper, I crab-crawl back. I recognize this place. The tree planted near my mom's grave. The stone angel a few rows away. It's Forest Hills Cemetery. My eyes dart around and I notice that something is off. It looks different. The colors are faded, muddled. Everything is a little out of focus, like I'm staring through a dirty glass. And there's this creepy fog that hovers almost as if it's lurking, waiting to attack.

Several rows over I see an elderly man walking toward his car. I race toward him. "Hello! Hey!"

He climbs inside and shuts the door. "Can you hear me?" I try to bang on the window, but my fist passes right through the glass. I gasp and yank my arm back. He starts up the engine. "Stop. Wait."

I run around to the front of the car and stare at him through the windshield. There's something different about him. He's blurry, like I'm looking at him through eyeglasses that are too strong.

He stares in my direction for a long moment. I believe I have his attention, then he shifts gears and drives forward. I cry out, expecting the pain of impact. But instead of being hit, the car passes right through me. My body tingles.

I glance down at myself. "How . . . What's happening?" I spin around and watch as the car rolls away. Is this a dream?

The wind rustles the dead leaves on the trees, and the sound it makes . . . it's like muffled crying.

"Wait! Please." I hurry after the car, desperate to find a way to communicate. I jog behind. "I'm right here!" I chase him outside the cemetery gates. He drives away, turning onto the main road.

Out of breath, I lean forward, my swollen hands on my knees. As I stand in the middle of the street, a thought makes me gasp aloud. The cemetery is close to Hyde's house. Maybe he'll be able to explain what's happening. I take off, running toward his junkyard.

With every step, I'm aware of this eerie presence around me. Like someone is watching, following my movements. I make the mistake of turning around and what I see causes me to stumble and fall. I hit the concrete hard.

"Justin."

I scramble to my feet.

My mom.

No. A grotesque version of my mom stands in the middle of the street.

Her too-big head is not centered on her body. One shoulder is higher than the other. Her limbs are not the same size or length. And her fingers . . . they're stretched long with nails as sharp as claws.

She's barefoot, wearing a blue hospital gown. Her body is thin, her skin that unhealthy gray color of sickness. Except for a few strands of long dark hair, her head is bald.

Three hundred and ninety-nine days now. That's how long it's been since she died. I've wanted to see her again, but not like this. *Never* like this.

She extends her arms toward me. "Come give me a hug, baby."

I blink hard to erase the vision in front of me, but she's still there. "One day soon you'll leave from here and fight against all you fear." That line from Zee's chant pops into my head. Everything I've experienced since I woke up in the coffin has been a fear. Dying. Now this. Reliving my mom's illness and death.

"Justin, I need you," the Not-Mom says. She stalks closer. I'm frozen in place. When I remain silent, her expression morphs into fury. "I said, come here."

I slowly back away. "You're not my mom."

She sneers. "I'm the only mom you'll ever know." She lifts her arms, forming a cradle. "Rock-a-bye, Justin, on a treetop. Your fears will keep coming and never stop. And when you break, the end will be near. This is your new home and the Seeker is here."

"Stop it! Stop." I slap my hands over my ears. "You're not real. You can't be real."

The wind moans and flutters the hospital gown around her frail body. Not-Mom ghosts five feet closer. Her movement is so fast she's a blur. She repeats that creepy chant.

Her cackling chases me as I race away. Not my mom. Not my mom. Just a nightmare. A living, breathing nightmare.

I slide to a stop in front of Hyde's home, falling into the chain fence. I spin around, terrified of what I might see, but there's no one there. That thing is gone, but for how long?

With weak arms, I push away from the fence and sluggishly make my way up the driveway past Hyde's ice cream truck. It's quiet, the kind of quiet that is unsettling and unnatural. As I walk forward, my gaze skates toward the backyard, where Quincy disappeared. It was just yesterday. I think. Who knows how long I was in that coffin before I woke up?

"Hyde," I call out as I reach the bottom of the front porch. My legs refuse to climb the steps. "Hyde!"

No response. A chill seeps through my clothing. "Hyde!" My voice is louder, angrier.

"He can't hear you," a voice says quietly.

I swivel around. A young girl stands behind me. Dirty, disheveled hair hangs to her shoulders. She wears a dingy white shirt with a faded rainbow across the front. Her fraying jeans are covered in different-colored patches. She's not out of focus like the old man was.

My breath catches in my chest. "You can see me? Who . . . who are you?"

"Nobody." Her brown eyes dart around and her fingers twist the tattered edges of her worn shirt. "We're all nobody here." She starts to back away.

"Wait! Don't go!" I rush forward and reach out to grab her arm.

With a cry, she flinches away. "Don't touch. Never touch," she says in a harsh whisper.

"I'm sorry. I . . ." I drop my hand. "Please don't go. The Seeker took me and . . ." My voice cracks. "Can you, will you help me?"

She shakes her head. "I tried to help before but . . ."

"What do you mean?"

"Doesn't matter," she says.

"I need to find my friends." I take a tentative step closer. "My name is—"

"Justin. And you want to find Lyric and Nia."

My jaw drops. "You know me? You know them? How? Have you seen them? Are they okay? Where are they? Can you take me to them?"

She watches me steadily as I fire off questions. "I don't know where they are."

Hisssss. I jump as several black birds streak across the sky.

They're not crows, but something scarier, larger. They circle above us, as if searching for prey to devour, making raspy hissing sounds.

"I have to go," she says, her eyes clouded with fear. "You should hide."

"Wait! How do you know me and my friends?"

She backs away. "I saw you before, with my brother."

I hurry after her. "Brother? Who's your brother?"

Her eyes harden as she points at the house. "Hyde."

I stumble to a stop. Everything in me shuts down. "Who are you?"

"I'm his sister, Mary," she says quietly. "The one he left behind."

18

"His sister," I say faintly, glancing back at the house.

She nods and her gaze continues to bounce around. Hyde has a sister. Was she the girl in the photo I saw at his house?

"He left you here?" Shock gives way to anger. I didn't think Hyde could get more foul. I was wrong.

Mary rubs her pale, thin arms and trembles. My eyes lock on her wrist. I step closer. "You're tagged, too?"

She extends her arm. "I played the game with him. I'm 233." A number is branded on her skin. "What are you?"

"I don't have a number. It's just a swirly mark."

Mary stares at me for a long moment. Her eyes are haunted. "For now. The mark turns into a number. You'll be counted, too."

I swallow hard. "Counted for what?"

Loud barking has me spinning around. Butch races from around the house, growling and snarling.

I stumble back and Mary dodges me so we don't touch.

"He can't hurt you," she says.

"Can he see us?"

"No, but he senses us like . . ." She falls silent as Hyde opens the front door and steps onto the porch. He stares in our direction with a smirk. My hands curl into fists.

"I know you're there," he says.

Mary steps forward and her face transitions from fear to disgust. "I'll always be here, Brother."

My gaze swings from her to Hyde. "It was you! He was talking to you. That's why he was acting so weird when we went to his house."

Mary picks at a scar on the back of her hand. It isn't completely healed. She mumbles something to herself.

I take a cautious step toward her. "Mary?"

"I distracted him. He wouldn't have let you inside and you needed to see."

"See what? The room with the pictures of the missing kids?"

She nods. "I hoped you'd find it. I thought it would help you figure out what was going on."

Butch runs up the stairs to stand next to his master. "Mary,

I wonder if you have someone with you now? Maybe a couple new friends?" Hyde smiles. "Justin, are you there?"

I'm so hot, I'm surprised I'm not shooting flames. "Yeah, I'm here," I say, though I know he can't hear me. "But not for long."

"The Seeker always gets what it wants," Hyde says.

Mary's hands curl into fists as she glares at her brother. "Because of your help."

Hyde tilts his head upward toward the sky. "Butch, let's go enjoy the sunshine."

"Sunshine?" I mutter. "It looks like we're about to have a storm."

"He doesn't see what we see," Mary says. "This place is a darker, scarier version of that world."

Hyde reaches inside and grabs a leash. After securing it on the dog's collar, they step off the porch and stroll down the driveway, right past where Mary and I are standing. Hyde whistles that eerie Seeker tune, the same as Zee's chant, as he leaves the junkyard. I want to run after him, yell at him for helping the Seeker, but there's no point. I need to focus on figuring out this place so we can escape.

"What do you mean by a version of that world? Hyde mentioned a place called Nowhere. Is that where we are?"

Mary opens her mouth to respond, then freezes. Her eyes widen, her chest rising and falling heavily. "Oh no."

"What is it?" I search the area, fearful that Not-Mom is back.

She turns and races toward the junkyard. I have no idea what she's running from, but I follow, weaving around the maze of rusted equipment in the yard. My backpack bounces against my back. She's fast and I struggle to keep up as my panic builds. After several twists and turns I lose track of her.

"Mary!" I slide to a stop, panting for breath. "Mary!"

"Here," she whisper-yells. I glance to my right to see her huddled behind an overturned refrigerator. She waves me over.

I slide behind the appliance, careful not to touch her. "What is it?"

"Rat snakes." She tucks her long hair behind her ears. Her hand trembles.

What?! "I didn't see anything." I keep my voice lowered to match hers.

"You wouldn't, unless you touch me. It's my fear." She pulls up her knees and wraps her bare arms around them. "That's why we never touch each other. My fears would become yours. And your fears would become mine."

I stare at her. Touching someone tags them with your worst nightmares. I can't handle my own. Dealing with someone else's . . . "Are they close?"

She tilts her head. "I don't hear them now, but I don't know. We should wait until I know for sure it's safe." Her lips tilt into a sad smile. "You'll be doing a lot of hiding here."

It's one big horrific game of Hide and Seek. And after seeing my Not-Mom, I'm guessing Mary is not dealing with a normal snake.

"What does it look like? I've never heard of a rat snake."

She swallows hard. "It's not . . . it's not the normal reptile. I'm afraid of rats and snakes. Here they're combined."

My mouth opens, then snaps closed. I don't know what to say.

She tugs up a pant leg. Bite marks cover her chewed-up calf and ankle. "They like to nibble on me."

I glance away and exhale a loud breath to hold back the queasiness bubbling inside me. I can't even . . .

For a long moment, I'm unable to speak and she seems okay with the silence.

"How long have you been here?"

"Nine years. I was seven when I was brought here. I was taken right after my brother."

Nine years. My head drops back against the file cabinet behind me. Hyde said he was in Nowhere for seven years and he's been back home for two.

"You played Hide and Seek together?" I ask.

"Yeah," she says bitterly. "There were a lot of kids playing and I don't even remember what rules we broke. When we got here, my brother promised to take care of me, said he'd get us home." She stares off in the distance. "He changed. He wasn't around when I needed him, then he wasn't around at all. One day he was back home and working for the Seeker."

"How did that happen?"

She's silent for a long time. "I don't know. Maybe he volunteered because he couldn't handle all the fears. Maybe the Seeker saw something in him, some weakness . . . I've thought about whether I would have made the same choice he did."

"And?"

"No," she says hesitantly. "I want to go home, but not like that."

"Mary, we're getting out of here. Me and my friends have a plan . . . well, sort of. We have backpacks." I gesture to mine. "We're hoping that the stuff inside can help us defeat the Seeker and escape this place."

"There's no escape."

"I don't believe that. There's a way here, there has to be a way out," I say.

Mary hugs her legs and focuses her dark gaze on me. Her expression is so fierce, it ages her. "Listen. You run. You hide. You stay safe when you can. That's it. Doing anything different is dangerous and stupid."

"I know you don't believe me, but we are going home," I say. "Tell me about this place."

Her eyes briefly close. When they focus on me again, I draw back. All I see is darkness and pain.

"It's like a shadow of our real world."

I cross my legs and shift toward her. "I don't understand."

She scoots back. "You know those paintings made up of different pictures?"

"A collage."

She nods. "That's what Nowhere is. Your personal fears and

nightmares are here and so are the places you're familiar with."

I look around. "So, it's like a giant puzzle? Kids brings in pieces of themselves and it all fits together to create this world?"

"Yeah, that's it. Hyde and his house are from my life. It's one of my . . . pieces."

And mine. I saw the cemetery because it was another personal place.

"It's a part of the never-ending nightmare," she says dryly. "Seeing home, but not *being* there."

That's why the old man at the cemetery looked weird and couldn't see me.

"Can you see all of my places?" I ask.

She nods. "It's a part of Nowhere now."

"You said 'we'? You've seen other kids?"

"You'll run into some when they're not hiding. We help each other if we can, but we never—"

"Touch," I say.

She nods.

My brain is still short-circuiting. "So earlier, a car drove right through me, but I'm leaning against this file cabinet. Shouldn't I fall through it?"

"No, it's . . ." She bites the corner of her mouth. "We can't interact with the real world."

I frown. "Still confused."

She picks up a stick and writes "Help" in the dirt. "You can see this but no one in the real world would. We're physically unable to communicate with them."

She touches the ground beneath us and the file cabinet behind me. "You're new so you still think of this as solid, but once you're here long enough you'll understand."

No way I'm waiting around for that.

She pushes her hand through a metal door. "See?"

"You can help us."

She shakes her head. "There's no way out unless you work for the Seeker like my brother."

My lips curl in disgust. "No way! Our friend—"

A whistling sound cuts through the air. I peek around the refrigerator to see Hyde strolling back up his driveway with Butch trotting beside him. My blood boils. He helped bring us to Nowhere and he needs to pay for his dirty deeds. He can't get away with this.

"Where are you going?" Mary asks.

I didn't even realize I was moving. "I'm going to find my friends and get us home." My hands tremble and I clench them into tight fists. "Are you coming?"

Mary stares at me, not blinking, for so long I get nervous. It's weird. I wait, fighting not to squirm under her intense gaze.

She climbs to her feet and brushes dirt off her hands. "My brother lied and told our father I ran away. I've watched my dad cry night after night."

"Hyde only cares about himself. He's proven that."

"I want some payback. If there's a chance you can help me with that, then I'm in."

I feel her on the revenge. "So where do we start looking?"

"First, we need Duke," she says.

"Duke?"

She weaves around the broken appliances until we reach the driveway. "He's been waiting for someone like you for a long time."

19

"What do you mean he's been looking for someone like me?" I wanted to bypass the cemetery, but Mary said this was the quickest way to where we'd find Duke. As we walk back, I notice how the locations transition into new ones. Some I recognize, others I don't.

My eyes skip around searching for any sign of Not-Mom. I'm still shaky from her last appearance.

The sky grumbles, the thunder loud and scary. Dark clouds, almost black, creep across the sky, muting the faint light from above. Mary's head pops up, and she skids to a stop. Her body trembles.

My stomach flutters. "Mary?"

Her gaze snaps to me. "What?" she barks.

I jerk back. She stares at me, but I'm not sure if she sees me. "Are you okay? What is it?"

She's quiet for a while, her eyes slowly regaining focus. "It's—" She shakes her head as if to clear it. "I thought—you just always have to expect terrible things here."

Like Not-Mom. She's around. Lurking. I tug on the straps of my backpack, making sure it's secure if I need to run.

Mary starts walking again. She stomps through the tall grass of the field we're crossing.

"Duke. How long have you known him?"

"A couple of years now. I hide. He hides." She shrugged. "We talk. It's been a while since I've seen him. Kids here don't really hang out together. You find your own way to deal and try not to draw attention."

"From the Seeker?"

She laughs, but it's not a funny sound. It's sad. "From anything."

I want to ask about the "anything," but I'm afraid to.

"I think Duke knows more about this place and the Seeker than anyone else here," she says.

We stop at the edge of some woods. It's crowded with tall trees with twisted trunks. Large clustered growths, like infected pimples, cling to the bark, and ropes of thick roots play Twister across the thirsty ground. A howling wind rustles the dead leaves. They shower down around us. I don't have a good feeling about this.

"Duke is in there?" I ask.

The temperature drops. Goose bumps sprout along my arms.

"Justin?" Not-Mom whispers.

I spin around, expecting to see that thing again. Nothing's there, but I sense this creepy presence hovering. The muscles around my chest tighten with dread.

"Not real," I whisper to myself. "Not real. Get out of my head."

"What is it?" Mary glances over her shoulder. She takes a step away from me as if whatever is wrong with me is contagious.

I can't share my nightmare with her. It's too personal. I slide my trembling hand into my pocket and grab the puzzle piece. I hear myself panting but can't seem to regulate my breathing. Inhale. Exhale.

Mary watches me. I draw back from her cool, blank stare. She resembles her brother—detached, emotionless—and that worries me. "Let's go."

She enters the woods and I cautiously follow. There's a narrow dirt path, maybe a running trail that winds through the cluster of deformed trees. Their tall warped trunks and branches cast a sinister spell. With each step, I question my decision to follow Mary. The deeper we trek into the woods, the more uneasy I become. Where is she taking me? Can I really trust her?

She makes a turn, taking us off the trail. We have to climb over tree stumps and thick brush. Branches scratch at my face and arms. Vines tangle around my ankles. Dead sticks snap and crunch as I stomp forward.

I'm about to turn around when we step out of the woods and into a small clearing near a pond. I spot a primitive shelter. It's built out of sticks. Mary stops at the edge of the open area.

I shift from foot to foot. "Mary?"

"Shhhhh," she says.

I wait. Then wait a little longer.

"It's safe," she says. "You can come out."

I step around her to see who she's talking to. There's no one there, only trees. Yep, this is bad. Time to roll out. I start planning my escape, when a boy emerges from the trees. My jaw drops. He was completely hidden.

Duke. I don't know what I was expecting. My eyes slowly scan him from head to toe—his white, thin face is spotted with dirt. His tangled black hair is shaved on one side, revealing a thick, long scar that runs from the corner of his right eyebrow to the back of his right ear. He wears dark, baggy pants that are wider at the top and narrow as they reach his ankles. Suspenders dangle from his waist, forming big loops that rest against his thighs. He's wearing brown ankle boots with laces.

It's clear from his clothing he's been here a long time.

He prowls closer, his movements jerky. His head is tilted at an angle like he's listening for something far away. His green eyes are locked on me, but it feels like he's aware of everything that is going on around him.

"What's this?" He clears his throat as if it's been a while since he's spoken. He nods in my direction.

"I brought someone to see you," says Mary.

"I'm Justin."

"Just-in," he says, like he's testing out my name. "Haven't met another Justin. There's a Brian. Carter. Matt. Jared . . . lots of others. No Justin."

Duke can't be much older than me. He's about my height and much slimmer. His collar bones can be clearly seen through his long-sleeve shirt.

"He has a backpack," Mary says, like that explains everything. "He says he's here to help everyone escape and to destroy the Seeker."

Duke's steps falter. "What?" He blinks hard, then rubs his arm across his eyes.

"We're real," Mary says, holding up her hands as if she's surrendering. "This isn't . . . We're not . . ."

When she falls silent, I peek over at her. She chews on her bottom lip. It suddenly hits me as I face Duke. He's worried we're a fear. Not real. Maybe something here to trick him.

Duke mumbles to himself, then focuses his attention back on me. "Give me your backpack."

"Why?" My grip tightens on the straps.

"I want to see what's inside." He waves his hand at me, motioning for me to hand it over. "Give it."

I glance at Mary. She nods as if to say, *It's okay.*

After a moment of hesitation, I slide my backpack off my aching shoulders and extend it out to him.

"No, no, no. On the ground," he says, with an eye roll.

Oh yeah. That whole not-touching thing. I set the backpack down.

He picks it up with mud-caked fingers. My hands twitch. I want to snatch it back from him.

"After a kid from our neighborhood was taken, me and my friends realized we could sneak in stuff that could help us defeat the Seeker."

Duke unzips the top pocket. "Flashlight, rope, matches, pocketknife . . . no, no, no."

Heat spreads through my body. "Lyric packed other tools—"

Duke laughs, it's loud and wild. "These are camping supplies. Junk. You really think this stuff can destroy the Seeker? Have you seen the monster? Seen what it can do? You have no idea—"

"Then tell me!" I say, throwing up my hands. "Mary thinks you can help. That you've been looking for a way to escape. Maybe the stuff we brought is stupid, but I don't care. I'm gonna do anything, use anything to find my friends and get us all home! If you don't want to help, fine. I'll figure it out myself." My heart is pounding as I glare at Duke.

Breathe. Breathe. Breathe. Sweat trickles down the side of my face.

He watches me, his head tilted to the side. I stuff my hand in my pocket to grab the puzzle piece. His eyes follow the movement.

"Duke, you know more about this place than us. You talked about gathering a group to defeat the monster." Mary nods toward me. "What if he and his friends can help? What if there is a way for us to finally go home?"

"Home," Duke says. He frowns like it's hard to imagine.

"You still want to escape, right?" I ask.

He scoffs. "Everyone wants to escape. That's not the problem. The Seeker has gotten stronger. The fears, so many fears . . . They're scarier and last longer."

Mary runs her fingers over the scar on her arm. "I've noticed it, too."

"There still has to be something we can do," I say.

Duke sets the backpack down and sits on a tree stump. His right leg bounces repeatedly. "You must be new."

"I got here today."

He smiles sadly. "Yep. That explains it. Totally explains it."

"What?" I ask.

"Why you make it sound so simple. You think you'll just find your friends and leave. No, no, no. That's not how this place works." He mumbles something under his breath.

I'm growing more and more frustrated the longer I talk to him. I need to find Nia and Lyric. "Help me understand. You know a lot, right? You've been here—"

"Eighty years," he says. "I've been here eighty years."

20

"Wait, what?!" No way I heard him right.

"Eighty years."

I gawk at him.

"I didn't realize it was that long," says Mary faintly.

Duke jumps to his feet and paces. His eyes dart around. "I've figured out a lot since I got here. You know the monster kidnaps kids who break the rules of Hide and Seek?"

"Uh, yeah." I shakily sit on the ground. My legs will no longer hold me. Eighty years.

"You're lucky. I had no idea what happened to me when I first arrived," Duke says. "Or why I was here."

I gasp. I never thought about the kids who have no idea their disappearances are tied to the game. All of a sudden . . . you're gone. Confronted by your fears with no one to help or explain why. That's horrible. Man, the stuff Duke has had to deal with . . . How did he survive? I've been here one day and can't handle it, but he's been here *eighty years*. What does that do to a kid?

"This place is much different than when I first arrived," he says, picking at the dirt underneath his nails. "So different."

"What do you mean?" I shift to find a more comfortable position on the ground.

"A long time ago, this world was an empty, dark space. I was . . . nowhere. Then one day the Seeker revealed itself." He stares off in the distance, his eyes empty.

"Duke?" I say after a long moment of silence.

He jolts, blinking hard. "What?"

I glance at Mary, then back to him. "You said the Seeker revealed itself. What happened then?"

Duke frowns. "Fear and pain," he says, like the answer is obvious.

A cold breeze whistles through the trees and a drop of rain hits my face, sliding down my cheek. "Should we be out in the open like this? Is the Seeker listening, watching?"

Duke gestures around the woods. "The monster is everywhere, everything."

I shudder as I remember the drawing I saw on Zee's and Hyde's walls, and what grabbed Nia. "The thing with the red eyes."

"So, you've seen it?" Duke says, an eyebrow raised.

I nod. "Where is it now?"

Duke stares up at the gray sky. "Not here. It's hunting again."

I swallow hard. "Another kid? How do you know?"

He taps his chest, then the side of his head. "I can feel the difference. When it's gone my heart beats right, and the noise in my head isn't so loud. But it can appear at any time. I have other hiding places, not just these woods, but it finds me. Always finds me. It lives off my fears, our fears."

"It's every scary thing you see." Mary hugs herself tight.

My heart skips a beat. "I don't understand."

"The more kids, the more fear, the stronger it becomes. When we touch or tag each other the terror is doubled. The Seeker gets more power. It—" Duke spins around and stares toward the woods.

"What—?" I jump to my feet as he races past me. He grabs a large stick off the ground and hurriedly draws a large circle around himself.

Mary and I exchange a horrified look. "Duke—"

"Shhhhhh." Breathing heavily, he raises the stick in the air as if he's preparing to hit something.

I spin around, searching for the danger, but there's nothing there. My heart is pounding so hard it echoes in my ears.

After a long moment, he slowly lowers the stick and tosses it aside. He turns to face us; his expression is blank. I wait to see if he will explain, but he remains silent.

"What just happened?" I ask.

"Something," he says. "But it's over for now. Safe in the circle."

I side-eye Mary. Is she sure Duke is the person we need to help us escape?

"What were we talking about?" he asks, clenching and unclenching his hands.

"You were explaining how the Seeker has more power because of all the kids in Nowhere," Mary says.

I slide my backpack on and tighten the straps. "How many kids are here?"

"Over three hundred at least," he says.

My eyes widen. "The last couple of days some of my friends were taken. Nia, Lyric, Quincy, Carla, and Shae. We've added to that."

Duke nods. "I knew you were coming. There's never been that many so close together. I felt the Seeker's power grow stronger."

"Justin still has the mark. No number yet," Mary says.

"You'll get one soon," he says. "It appears shortly after you arrive."

I search for the mark on Duke's wrist. From the angle he's holding his arm, I only see the one, and not the rest of the number. One hundred and something. Wow.

I gulp. The thought of being numbered is terrifying. I'll officially be the Seeker's. I won't be Justin—just whatever number I'm given.

Suddenly, a memory hits me so hard I gasp. A sense of dread worms its way through my body. "Four hundred."

Duke frowns. "What are you talking about?"

Oh man! It's all starting to make sense. Every piece of the puzzle is snapping into place. "My friend Zee—"

"You can't believe anything he says. He's a traitor, like my brother," Mary says with a glare.

"Zee escaped," I say.

Mary scoffs.

"No one has ever escaped." Duke eyes me suspiciously.

I pace. "Listen, Zee made it out somehow. I don't know how but he did. He was messed up when he got back, but he tried to warn us about the Seeker. He would say weird stuff, like riddles. It was something like, 'Four hundred is the special number, to release it from its world of slumber.'"

"You can't trust him!" Mary cries.

I spin around and glare at her. "You don't know him. I do. He's my friend."

"So, that means he can't lie?" she asks.

"He wouldn't lie to me."

"Wait. Just stop. Let me think." Duke touches the scar on the side of his head. "Four hundred is the special number, to release it from its world of slumber," he repeats slowly. "And Zee was talking about the Seeker?"

I nod. "Yeah, had to be."

"You're not going to listen to this, are you?" Mary says to Duke. "We can't trust anything Zee said. He was—"

"I'm telling you, Zee was trying to help. His riddles mean something."

"What else did he say?" Duke's focus is so intense on me, I flinch.

"He said, 'Once it reaches its final goal, with the power that it stole, it will win and now can roam. Our world becomes its seeking home.'"

"Its seeking home," Duke says slowly, with a frown. "Its. Seeking. Home."

"Yeah and . . ." I freeze. "Oh no!"

"What is it?" Mary asks warily.

I run a trembling hand over my face. The thought is so horrible it takes me a moment to form the words. "This is the Seeker's world, right? But what if, what if it wants to leave?" I ask. "*Our world* becomes *its* seeking home."

Duke falls back. "What . . . You think . . . ?"

"You say it's getting stronger. It brings us here to feed off our fear, but what if it's so strong now that it can leave?" I say.

Mary's hand flies up to cover her mouth.

"Our friend Shae, she was taken from camp a couple of days ago. But there was *another* Shae at Zee's party, around the same time, acting really weird. She's the one who suggested we play Hide and Seek. We think it was the Seeker pretending to be her. That means the monster is able to leave Nowhere, for at least a little while, right?"

"You think the count is leading up to the *Seeker's escape*?" he asks.

"What if four hundred kids are the key? The key to free the Seeker from Nowhere. Like to give it the power to cross over to the real world and stay permanently."

All color drains from Duke's face. "No, no, no. That can't happen."

"No kid would be safe," says Mary with wide eyes.

Duke swings around, his arms flailing. "I was so busy hiding . . . I missed the signs. All this time it had a plan and I didn't see it. It used to be only a few kids arrived a year, but over time, more and more have appeared in Nowhere. Faster. Sometimes multiple at once."

"Like me and my friends," I say.

And the Seeker wasn't working alone anymore either. He had help from Hyde.

"It's been taking more kids, unleashing more terrors, gaining power," says Duke, clutching his head. "And now—"

I cry out as a stinging pain radiates up my arm. The swirly mark begins to shift on my skin. A three appears. Then a nine. Then another nine. Three hundred and ninety-nine.

My eyes fly to Duke and Mary. Their expressions reflect the terror clawing at my heart.

If the Seeker is trying to reach four hundred, it's now only one kid away.

21

"I have to find my friends. We don't have much time left," I say. "The Seeker could get that last kid any time now."

"But how do we stop it?" Mary asks. "It's too powerful."

"We can figure it out on the way." I spin around, searching for the way out through the woods. The most important thing is to find Lyric and Nia. I made a promise.

"Justin."

I get goose bumps. It's Not-Mom's eerie voice. My gaze jumps around the wooded area. I don't see her, but I *feel* her. It's a dark, suffocating presence.

"You can't leave me, baby," Not-Mom whispers. The wind carries her voice to me and her haunting voice tugs at my heart. I reach for the puzzle piece in my pocket and freeze.

Three hundred and ninety-nine. I stare at the mark on my wrist. Not only is it my number, it's the amount of time since I've seen my mom. Three hundred and ninety-nine days.

My legs wobble. It feels like I'm being split in two.

"Justin?" Duke says.

My head pops up. I stare at him through watery eyes. Chest hurts. Hard to breathe. One, two, three, four. The loud thuds of my heart echo in my head.

"I have to find my friends."

A panic attack in front of my friends is different than having one in front of strangers. I feel weak and helpless. This is not the image I need to project to get people to help me defeat the Seeker.

"That . . ." Duke points at me, his eyes pained. "Whatever just happened, it's going to get worse. More intense. Scarier for all of us if we go after the Seeker."

I swallow hard. "I can deal if it means at the end we go home."

He looks down, mumbling to himself. "We could stop it. No more fear. Safe again."

I watch him wrestle with his thoughts.

He finally lifts his head. "I'll help."

Mary wrings her hands. "Me too."

This is good. The best I could hope for. We're forming a team.

Now I need to find the rest of the players—Nia, Lyric, Quincy, Carla, and Shae.

"Where do we go now?" asks Mary.

"I'll lead us out of the woods, then Justin can direct us toward an area where his friends might be. Something familiar to them," Duke says.

He slowly gazes around the area; his weary eyes briefly land on the pond and the shelter he built out of sticks. I can't imagine what he's thinking right now. If things go like we hope, this will be the last time he ever has to hide.

He exhales a loud breath, then marches into the woods. We follow him through the maze of trees. I'm immediately uneasy as we push past the low-hanging limbs and thick brush.

The magnitude of what we're facing hits me in waves, threatening to drown me. My legs are a little unsteady. All the emotions and stress of the day are catching up to me, but I have to keep moving. No time to rest now.

A giggle bubbles up inside and I can't hold it back. I randomly think about my counselor. Man, will I have a lot to talk to her about. Those are gonna be some interesting sessions. I clear my throat to hold back another giggle and ignore the weird glances from Duke and Mary. They must think I'm cracking under the pressure. I don't blame them.

When we finally reach the path and follow it back into the park, I breathe a little easier. We leave the shadows of the tall trees and step into the hazy, gloomy environment around us. The silence is creepy. Dark clouds crowd the sky and the constant mist adds to the murkiness.

Duke shifts from foot to foot as his eyes zip around. "Different," he says. "Not like my woods."

"Which way do we go now?" Mary asks when we hit a cross street.

I recognize this area; it's a few miles from where home should be. "You said somewhere familiar, right? We should try my neighborhood first."

We walk down the sidewalk. A girl stands on the corner holding a small dog. Their blurry forms flicker in and out like the old man I saw in the cemetery. The dog growls and barks loudly as we stroll past it. It wiggles around, almost jumping out of her arms. She may not be aware that we're here, but the dog is. Just like Hyde's dog, Butch.

"Duke—"

"Don't talk." He glances back over his shoulder.

"What?" I ask.

"I need to listen. Watch," he says.

I glance at Mary. She searches the area like Duke.

"We're not alone," he says. "Keep moving."

My stomach drops. I don't see anything, but that doesn't mean much. Not here. I quicken my pace, but can't outrun the panic swirling inside me. What's out there? What does it want?

We hurry through town. With every turn, I'm hoping to see one of my friends. I have to find them. I don't know what I'll do if I don't.

"Hey!" a boy's voice yells out. "Where'd you go?"

I freeze. I know that voice. "Lyric?" I spin around, trying to see around the buildings. I only see blurry forms of people in the distance. Where is he?

"Wait! I'm right here," a girl calls out. "Stop!"

I gasp. That's Nia! They're close.

"Who is that?" Mary asks.

"It's Lyric and Nia!"

I start moving in the direction of their voices. Duke blocks my path. "Wait. It could be a trick."

"No, it's them. I know it. I have to find them." As I start to go around him, he cries out and stumbles back.

"What is it? What's wrong?" Mary says, staring at him with wide eyes.

Duke's body twitches as he frantically pats his clothes. "It burns! It burns!"

He falls to the ground and rolls around, shouting in pain.

My heart skips. I realize what's happening. He's on fire!

I reach for him, but he says, "Don't touch me! Don't touch me!"

Coughing, he covers his nose and mouth as if trying to avoid smoke. His skin reddens and welts appear on his face.

"What do we do?" Mary asks.

My stomach turns as I watch him flail around. I should help, but . . . I hesitate. Suddenly a stream of water shoots past me.

I spin around. Lyric holds a blue-and-yellow water blaster. Water douses Duke until his clothing is wet. He groans and collapses onto his back. His chest rises and falls with heavy, labored breaths.

"Are you okay?" Lyric asks. "No more burning?"

Gasping, Duke nods. Mary kneels near him, but doesn't touch him.

My mind is struggling to process what just happened. Duke was on fire. Lyric is here and he has a water blaster.

"Lyric?"

He doesn't respond. It's as if he doesn't realize I'm here.

Frowning, Mary glances at me, then back at Lyric. "Don't you see him?"

He lowers the water blaster. "Who? The dude on the ground?"

A chill slides down my spine.

"No. Justin," Mary says, pointing at me.

"What—" He sucks in a loud breath and his eyes fly back to where I'm standing. "Justin?" His voice shakes. Trembling, he squeezes his eyes shut.

"Why can't you see me?" I ask.

"He's here. Justin is here. He found me," Lyric mutters to himself. "*He's here.* It's okay."

"Lyric . . ."

He doesn't respond to my voice. His chest rises and falls heavily. His hands are clenched at his sides.

I spin to Mary. "Ask him . . . ask him if he brought his harmonica."

She frowns. "What?"

"It's a thing. He'll understand."

"Justin wants to know if you brought your harmonica," Mary says hesitantly.

Lyric's eyes pop open and widen. They're bright with tears. His gaze lands on me, and he blinks hard several times. He *sees* me.

I swallow the giant lump in my throat.

"Justin," he says with a wobbly smile. "Man, I—"

"Lyric!" Nia races around the corner of the building. "Why didn't you answer me?" Panting, she stumbles to a stop when she spots me.

"Nia?" Lyric says in awe.

My heart pounds so hard in my chest it's hard to catch my breath. It slowly hits me. I've found them. They're safe. We're together again.

For a moment we stare at each other, then everyone is moving at the same time. I rush toward them. We're a couple of feet apart before I remember the danger. I stumble back away from them. "No! Don't touch me!"

22

They freeze, their eyes wide with shock.

"Justin, what's wrong?" Nia walks closer with her arms extended toward me.

I cringe and take several unsteady steps back. There's no way I want them to see Not-Mom, to experience what I'm going through.

"Dude, are you okay?" asks Lyric.

I have to take a couple of breaths before I can respond. "If we touch, we'll share our fears. You'll have mine and I'll have yours."

Nia gasps.

"Whoa," says Lyric. "Just when I thought it was impossible to hate this place more than I already do . . . BAM. The Seeker does the impossible."

Nia smiles weakly. "Well, I'm happy to see you, even if we can't hug."

"Same." Lyric's blue eyes look bigger with the dark smudges underneath them.

All I could think about was reuniting with them, but this is not how I hoped it would go down. We're close, but they still feel far away. The fear of touching keeps us apart. I look them over. Their clothing is ripped and dirty. What have they been through? And why couldn't Lyric see me?

"Who are you?" Lyric asks, staring over my shoulder. "What did I roll up on?"

Duke struggles to his feet. His wet clothing is plastered to his frail body. There are blistered burn scars on his cheeks and neck. Mary stands by his side.

Nia slides closer to Lyric. "Stranger danger."

"That's Duke and Mary. They're . . ." I pause. What are they? "They're on our side. I met up with them a while ago. They were kidnapped, too."

Nia still eyes them suspiciously. "Why is he wet?"

I wince.

Lyric shoves his water blaster back inside his backpack. "He was—"

"That's the sixth," Duke answers, examining the burns on the back of his hands.

"What?" asks Nia.

"I was on fire." He looks at Lyric. "Thanks for shooting water on me with that thing."

"Anytime." Lyric grimaces. "I mean, glad I could help, but I hope I don't have to do it again."

"Why, uh, why were you on fire?" Nia asks Duke.

"It's one of my fears, one of the ways the Seeker torments me." He squeezes water from his shirt. "Fire is number six, but there's more. Nine, I think. No, eleven. Definitely eleven."

"Uh, Duke has been here a long time. Eighty years," I explain to Lyric and Nia.

Their jaws drop.

"You're new. I'm not." Duke walks a short distance away and stares in the direction we came from. "We need to go. Move now. We shouldn't be in the open like this. There's . . . something. It's getting closer."

"I don't see anything," says Nia. "Are you sure?"

"I know. I feel it. I always feel it," Duke says, rubbing his temples. "We're not safe. Never safe."

"Justin, we found your friends. Now what?" Mary asks.

"We're still missing Carla, Quincy, and Shae." I start walking, heading in the direction of our neighborhood. I'm not sure where they'd go, but it's my best guess. "We need to find them, too, before we go home. That's the plan."

"Keeping it simple and scary," says Lyric. "Gotcha. Let's do it, then, because I'm not feelin' this whole 'almost real, but extra-scary world' thing."

"Parallel world or multiverse, if you want to be specific," Nia says, as she and the others follow. "If it wasn't a creepy place created by a monster, it'd be kinda cool if you think about it. Scientists debate about the existence of other universes and we're stuck in the proof that one exists." She brightens slightly. "Doesn't this make you think about other stuff? What if aliens are real? Or Bigfoot? Or the Loch Ness Monster?"

"The Kraken is totally real. That's why I don't swim in open water. Pools only for me," says Lyric with a grimace.

So happy we're back together. I'm not me without them. I reach out my hand to bump fists with Lyric, then remember we can't touch. I jerk back. He catches my gesture.

"Mental fist-bump," he says. "We'll save the real thing for when we get home."

"Okay."

"Mental hugs, too," Nia adds. "And, Justin . . . thanks for keeping your promise."

"Yeah, dude," says Lyric. "You found us like you said you would."

I nod because my throat is too tight to speak. They don't get it. I *had* to find them. There was no other option.

We walk awhile in silence before Lyric asks, "You sure we can trust Duke and Mary?"

His voice is lowered so only Nia and I hear him.

I peek over my shoulder. Duke's head is swiveling left and right as he takes in everything around him. It's clear he's uncomfortable being away from his woods.

"I think so. He wants to go home, too. He's been here forever. I can't even imagine what he's seen and been through."

"What about Mary?" Nia asks.

It hits me that I haven't told them. "Mary is Hyde's *sister.*"

Lyric's eyes widen. "You're lyin'!"

Nia trips over her feet. I have to weave to avoid running into her. "Is she dangerous, too?" she asks.

"No. I don't think so." I glance back at Duke and Mary. They're far enough away that they can't hear us, but not too far that we'd lose them. "Hyde left her here." I fill them in on everything Mary shared about Hyde and his dirty deeds. "And she's actually been helping us. Even before we got here. She distracted him while we were at his house. Remember how he was acting strange and we thought he was talking to himself?"

"It was her?" asks Lyric.

"Yeah, he couldn't see her but knew she was there."

"Wow," Lyric says with a shake of his head. "Man, this is all so unbelievable. I would pinch myself to make sure I'm awake, but I've already experienced too much pain. Side note." He gestures over his shoulder. "Backpack, yay!"

My lips tilt into a little smile. "Yeah, something went as planned."

"Moving too slow," Duke says. "We need to hurry. Which way do we go now?"

"This way." Through the mist, I recognize the strip mall. It's the same one we stopped at when we were searching for Hyde. Thunder rumbles. We walk faster.

"Justin was updating us," Lyric says to Duke. "We need to know what's going on so we can help."

"And I didn't even get to this." I hold up my wrist to show them the number branded on my skin.

Lyric extends his arm. "Yeah, I was wondering about that." He's number 398.

"I'm guessing this is a bad thing, huh?" Nia's wrist is tagged with 397.

I trade glances with Duke and Mary. We were right about the count. I was the last to arrive so my number is the highest.

"You remember Zee's creepy chant? He was counting and then he mentioned the number four hundred," I say.

Nia nods. "What about it?"

Lyric runs a palm over his face. "Wait. Let me guess. Is it a countdown to some big, freakin' evil apocalypse or something?"

"We believe if the Seeker captures four hundred kids, it might be able to leave Nowhere and go to the real world for good," Duke says.

Lyric throws up his arms. "Are you serious? The worst keeps getting worser."

"We're the key to the monster's escape," Nia says. "Not happy about that."

Mary lets out a whimper and skids to a halt.

"I knew it," Duke says.

She trembles and stares at something in the distance.

"What—?" I ask.

Suddenly, she bolts across the street.

Duke takes off after her. Lyric, Nia, and I follow. We don't move as fast because this is still new to us. We take time to dodge stuff even though there's no reason to.

"Mary!" Duke yells.

Up ahead, in a grocery store parking lot, she falls to the ground. She screams and is dragged across the pavement. We skid to a stop a few feet away from her. She's kicking and fighting her invisible foe, her fear.

"What's happening?" asks Nia.

"Her fear," I say, panting.

Lyric is out of breath and flushed. He makes a move like he's going to help.

"Stay back," says Duke.

Mary's body is tossed around like she's a rag doll.

"We wait until it's over. You touch her and it's your fear, too." Duke watches her with haunted eyes. "Never touch."

Mary's cries make my skin crawl. Bite marks and scratches appear on her arms.

"Screw this," says Lyric. "Friends don't let friends face their fears alone."

"She's not your friend," Duke says, but Lyric is already racing toward Mary. Nia is right on his heels. I hesitate. I want to help, but touching her means she'll know about my mom.

Mary curls up in a ball, whimpering. Lyric pulls her back and tries to help her stand.

"Oh, c'mon! This is ridiculous!" Lyric yells.

"What?" I yell, taking a few steps closer, then back.

"Rat. Snakes. The body is a snake, but it has legs, too. It's brown, with fur and scales, and like ten feet long," he cries.

"There's another one!" cries Nia.

I glance back at Duke. He's frozen.

Suddenly, Lyric is yanked forward and hits the ground hard. Scratches appear on his arms as he covers his face.

"Justin!" Nia pulls at his legs while also trying to free Mary.

Gotta help! I frantically pull off my backpack and fumble to open it. Maybe there's something inside that will stop the rodent-reptiles.

"Ahhh!" Lyric yells. He and Mary are tugged farther across the parking lot.

"No!" says Nia.

I don't think. I jump up and race toward them. The moment I touch Mary, a bolt of energy zips through me. Mary's pain is my pain. I blink and the rat snakes appear. I see them. Their furry heads rotate in my direction. And they see me.

The creatures let out a high-pitched noise, chittering and hissing. They're excited. I stagger back. They're communicating. The rodent-reptiles fix their fiery eyes on me. They have a new chew toy.

23

Lyric kicks free, scrambles to his feet, and tries to drag Mary to safety. "They're gonna attack again."

"Duke, grab my backpack. Look for something to help."

He paces back and forth, clutching his head, mumbling to himself. "More power when you fight back. It feeds off your fear."

"What?" Lyric yells. "Man, do something!"

The rat snakes move toward us in a slithering motion.

Nia moves so suddenly the loss of her grip on Mary causes us to stumble. She tugs something out of her pocket and stalks forward.

"Nia!"

She extends her arm and a mist envelops the rat snakes. Their pained squeaks make me wince. The rodent-reptiles crawl over each other in an attempt to escape. They stagger away chittering and hissing until they disappear.

Nia spins on her heels and holds up the canister triumphantly.

"What just happened?" Lyric says with wide eyes.

"I used the pepper spray from my keychain," Nia says. She looks just as shocked as I feel.

"Did you know it's not just for self-defense against humans? It can be used on attacking dogs, bears, and, apparently, giant, freaky rat snake things."

My mouth falls open. "The water blaster!" There was so much going on before I didn't even think about what it meant. I turn to Lyric. "You used the water blaster on Duke. And the pepper spray worked . . . We were right. The stuff we snuck in *can* help us!"

"Dude, we just leveled up," says Lyric. "This is a total game changer."

I was too busy running from my mom to even think about using something from my backpack to help me. I'm not sure what would work, but knowing we have weapons is amazing.

Lyric helps Mary stand. Wobbling, she tugs her arm away.

"You shouldn't have done that. Touch me, I mean," she whispers. "But thanks."

He rocks back on his heels. "Yeah, well . . . we couldn't let those things take you, but now you have our fears to battle, too." He winces. "Apologizing in advance."

"Me too," says Nia.

Since I touched Mary, she'll see Not-Mom. She'll *know*. The way things are going, everyone may know.

"Hey, Duke, thanks for all the help. Not." Lyric wipes blood off his arms.

Duke flinches and drops his head. "Eighty years. So many fears," he mumbles. "Too many. I don't want any more. I can't handle any more. You don't understand. You don't feel them all, see them all."

I didn't help at first. Did they notice? I reach into my pocket for the puzzle piece. I feel Nia's gaze on me, but I refuse to look her way. Must breathe.

"We always have each other's backs," Lyric says.

"And now we have to have Duke's, too." Nia gestures at everyone. "Did you know a team is a group of people coming together for one common goal? That's us now. We're in this together."

"No." Duke backs away. "This was a bad idea. I'm going back to—"

"Hiding?" Lyric asks. "There's no way I can do that forever, be trapped in this nightmare life."

"It's called survival. You could do it if you had to," Mary says quietly.

"Yeah, but the thing is," says Lyric with a quick glance at me and Nia, "I don't think you have to anymore. We're here now. We can help."

"And what if you make things worse?" Mary asks. "Things can always get worse."

"Or . . ." Nia says. "Things could get much, much better. Like 'defeat the Seeker, destroy Nowhere, go home' better."

"We're gonna either win or lose. I think our odds are fifty-fifty, probably a little less," Lyric says, smiling like he's gifted us with the best Christmas present ever.

Duke crosses his arms. "That doesn't sound good."

"Having two outcomes doesn't mean it's fifty-fifty. That's not how odds work," Nia says.

Lyric rolls his eyes. "Well, it's not *zero*."

"You in or not?" I ask Duke. "And I mean really in?" We need to get moving. Time is ticking and the Seeker is out there stalking its final victim. We're gonna face some crazy stuff. I need him to be solid.

Duke's weary eyes shift around, then land on me. "We have to stop the Seeker. For good. I'm in. There's no turning back now."

Lyric offers his fist for Duke to bump. "Go Team Terror."

Duke gives Lyric an "are you serious?" look.

I turn to Mary. She's staring in the direction where the rat snakes disappeared. Her eyes are troubled. "Mary, you're still with us, too, right?"

She blinks. "Even after all this time it takes a while to shake it off."

I get it. I don't hear Not-Mom but her icky presence is stuck to me.

Mary stands up straighter, pushing her shoulders back. "I'm still in."

Lyric claps his hands. "Okay, let's do this."

We're back on the move. We're determined, but still on edge. Anything could happen at any time. The dark sky grumbles, leaking more cold rain drops. The mist is thick and heavy, almost like a weight to slow us down. There's a constant feeling that something is lurking, preparing to attack.

"I know you're there," Duke mumbles.

"Who!?" Nia spins around.

Duke holds a finger to his lips. "Shhhhh. You're too loud. I spotted someone following us. Not too close. Not too far. Hidden, but there."

My heart pumps faster. Inhale. Exhale. "Someone, like a kid? Or something scary?"

Lyric tightens the straps on his backpack. "There are a lot of kids here. Shouldn't we run into more of them anyway?"

Duke mutters, gazing behind us. "Keep going for now," Duke says, walking again. "Pretend you don't know something is wrong."

Lyric snorts. "Uh, not possible."

I'm even more anxious now. We climb up the hill near the library and make our way back down, around the hospital. A siren blares in the distance. The sound echoes; it's ominous.

"Cold." Nia rubs her arms.

I stop and pull out the jacket I packed from my backpack. I'm chilly, but she's trembling.

She hesitates, staring at it, then back to me.

"Here," I say. "I know you're cold."

"Did I say that?" she asks.

I hesitate. "Yeah. And you're rubbing your arms."

She blinks, her gaze sort of confused. "Oh," she mumbles.

"You okay?"

"Yeah." She smiles, but it appears forced. She carefully takes the jacket, without touching, and walks away.

"Ahhhhhhh," someone screams.

I spin around. A kid runs down the street toward us. He's swinging his arms wildly. "Get off! Get off!"

"That's the one that's been following us," Duke says, backing away.

"They're biting me!" the kid yells. He dances around, brushing off his clothes.

He runs a little closer. Stops and stomps his feet. "Take that. And that. Stay away."

"Is that . . . ?" Nia peers in the distance.

I gasp. "Quincy!"

24

I run in his direction, then skid to a halt when I get a good look at him. It's like he's wearing a horror movie mask. There are welts all over his face and his left ear is twice as swollen as his right.

"What the—" Lyric stops beside me.

Panting, Quincy jogs closer. I lift up my hands to hold him back. He stops and leans forward with his hands resting on his knees. His backpack slips sideways, almost falling off.

"Quincy?" asks Nia, who now stands at my side.

He raises his head, and I flinch. It's painful to look at him.

"I didn't know if it was really you." He drops to the ground. "I—"

"Man, what happened?" Lyric asks as Duke and Mary approach us.

"Are you okay?" It's a stupid question. Obviously, he is far from okay. He's swelling up.

"B-b-bugs." Quincy's voice shakes and he breaks down. He's crying and shaking so hard his entire body is vibrating.

My jaw drops. "What kind of bugs could do this?"

Lyric turns to me and lowers his voice. "I recognize this is not the best time, and I'm all kinds of wrong considering I was just all about being a team player and helping others, but I hope I don't have to touch Quincy."

I grimace. *Me too.*

"Lyric!" says Nia.

"I'm being honest. Of course, if he's in danger I'll step up." Lyric peeks over his shoulder at Quincy and winces. "It's just . . . look at him."

"Do either of you have something in your backpacks that may help?" Nia asks.

"I brought a small first-aid kid. Maybe there's something we can use." I search inside the front pocket as Nia kneels next to Quincy. She's close, but not too close.

I find a small tube of ointment for burns and cuts. This might help.

"Is this another one of your friends?" Duke tilts his head to the side and studies Quincy.

"Yeah," I say.

Mary's seen Quincy before.

"We just need to find Carla and Shae now," says Nia.

Quincy cries out. I turn back to see him rubbing the ointment on his face. On his wrist, his mark is now the number 396. Just more confirmation we're right about the numbering.

"Is it helping?" I ask.

"A little. The bites aren't burning as bad. It felt like my face was on fire."

"Burning?" Lyric mutters. "Man, how did this happen?"

Quincy's hand freezes mid-motion, then slowly lowers to his side. "I, uh, there was a giant bee-nest-hive thing in a maze. It was full of different kinds of bugs. I finally got out, but they were chasing me. I thought I got away, but more bugs found me, and they were worse than the other ones—they were beetle-like with scorpion tails. And the buzzing sound they made hurt my ears."

Lyric's head jerks around as if he's searching for a swarm that could descend upon us.

"Quincy, have you seen Carla?" I ask anxiously.

His shoulders droop. "No. I've been looking for her and Shae."

"Where could they be?" Lyric asks.

Duke steps away, putting more distance between himself and the rest of the group. He crosses his arms tightly across his chest. "Something is changing. Do you feel it? We're wasting time. We need to go."

Quincy frowns, glancing from Duke to Mary.

"It's okay. They're with us," says Nia. "They want to help."

Quincy wipes more cream on his face. It leaves white streaks down his brown skin. "I was going to look at the park by my house. The one with the big tree fort."

I know that one. It also has a small area where they put on outdoor concerts. Me, Zee, my mom, and Mrs. Murphy saw some bands play there.

"If something ever happens and we get separated, that's where me and Carla meet up," Quincy says.

"That's not too far," says Lyric.

Nia reaches to pull Quincy to his feet, then snatches her hand back.

"What is it?" he asks.

"We can't touch." She shifts from foot to foot. "If we do, we'll share our fears. You'll get mine, and I'll get yours."

His eyes widen. I think he might start crying again, but he pulls it together. He slowly stands and even with the welts and cream on his face I see his determination. "We're gonna find Carla. She'll know what to do. She'll get us home." He marches in the direction of the park, his backpack bouncing against his back.

"Carla's gonna save us?" Lyric mumbles as we follow. "Maybe there was some kind of venom in those bug bites that is affecting his brain."

I hold back a laugh. Thunder booms. My humor quickly fades

away. A deep, growling sound echoes around us. Our gazes jump around, searching for incoming danger, but nothing emerges.

Quincy takes the lead, moving swiftly down the street. I catch some of Lyric and Mary's conversation as they walk beside me. "So, I meant to ask before but more scary stuff happened. Why rat snakes?"

Mary is quiet for a long moment. "When I was five, I was visiting my grandpa on his farm," she finally says softly. "I fell down an old well. It was dark and cold, half full from the rain. Rats and snakes were floating inside, some dead and some . . . not."

Quincy glances over his shoulder. His eyes are wide. His foot catches an edge of the concrete on the sidewalk, uplifted by a thick tree root. He regains his balance and his head snaps forward, but I can tell he's still eavesdropping.

Everyone waits for her to continue. The silence is tense.

"It was hours before my grandpa found me and the rats . . . They were hungry," she says.

I swallow the massive lump in my throat. Even when we leave here, I don't think I'll ever forget that story and what Mary's fear looks like.

Lyric expels a loud breath. "Yeah, I can see how that could be traumatic. Can I ask you something else?"

Duke mutters something that I can't make out.

"Yeah," Mary says reluctantly. She stops and turns to Lyric. The rest of the group halts, too.

"So . . ." Lyric looks at me, then back to Mary. "We touched you, so that means the rat snakes are coming for us. Just so I'm, uh, prepared. What happens next?"

Mary tucks her dark hair behind her ears. "What do you mean?"

"Well, it looked like they were taking you somewhere," Lyric says.

She stares at the cracked sidewalk. "To the well. They always take me back to the well."

Nia's hands fly up to cover her mouth. My stomach seesaws so violently I get nauseous.

"I have to crawl back out. I run. Hide. If they catch me, it all happens again." Mary's haunted eyes slowly rise and focus on Lyric. "And again. And again. That's what you can expect."

The color drains from his face. His mouth opens, then closes with a pop. "Oh."

"No more touching. No more touching," Duke mumbles.

It's not something I want to do, but I get a feeling we won't be given a choice by the time this is all over.

We're at the intersection of Olive Street and Brainard Road. One direction will take us to the park, the other way is home. My feet are glued to the ground.

"Justin?" Nia has stopped next to me.

"Why are we not moving?" Quincy asks. "We're almost there."

The sudden need to see Victoria wells up inside me. "I want to . . . I have to . . ."

Nia and Lyric stare at me for a moment, then nod. I need to go home.

"We're making a detour," says Lyric, walking quickly to my side. We head down the street.

"What?" Duke swivels his head from side to side. "Why?"

"There's someone I want to see," I say.

As we get closer, I notice a police cruiser parked in front of my house. Victoria stands in the driveway with an officer. He's short and muscular, with buzz-cut brown hair peppered with gray.

"You have to do something!" she says.

I'm not even aware I'm running toward her until I hear Nia yell my name.

"Officer Green, my brother is missing," Victoria says.

I skid to a halt in front of her. "Vic—"

She walks right through me and I shudder.

"It's been less than twenty-four hours," the officer says. "He could be off with his friends somewhere. They're probably all together."

They know about Nia and Lyric, too?

"He wouldn't do that. He wouldn't," she cries. Her clothes are wrinkled and her eyes are red. "*I'm* telling you something is wrong. I know Justin. He wouldn't run off, he wouldn't leave." She places her hand over her heart.

"I wouldn't leave you unless something made me, Vic," I whisper hoarsely.

"And what about my mom's room? It was trashed. Justin wouldn't have done that. That means there was a struggle, right? Maybe someone came into the house and took him."

"You said his mom died recently; maybe he's still dealing with the loss. He could have gotten upset and acted out—"

"No!" says Victoria. "And it was over a year ago."

Three hundred and ninety-nine days. My eyes are drawn to the mark on my wrist.

Victoria's hands interlock under her chin as if she's praying. "You have to believe me."

"Ma'am, I promise we're looking into it. We're canvassing the neighborhood, talking to people, but more than likely he'll show up soon." The cop hands her his card. "Call me if anything changes."

I stand beside Victoria, watching the officer get into his car and drive away. She buries her face in her hands.

"I'm sorry, Vic," I whisper brokenly.

She lifts her head and half turns in my direction. For a moment I think she hears me, but then she asks, "Where are you, Justin?"

My heart aches. "I'm right here."

With a sigh, she walks inside the house. It looks even more lonely than usual. Victoria is inside the emptiness. And that's how I feel. Empty.

Nia stares down the street toward her house. Her family is probably worried about her, too. "You want to go—"

"No," she says, biting her lip. "I don't want them to, uh, *not* see me, if that makes sense."

It does.

Duke sucks in a loud breath. He taps his chest, over his heart, then touches the side of his head. "We shouldn't have stopped. I knew it."

"What's wrong?" I say.

"Shhhhhh," he says frantically. "Need to find . . ." He starts mumbling to himself.

My heart rate skyrockets.

"No!" He takes off, sprinting away from us. We chase him.

"Duke!"

There is a strategy to his movement. He weaves around objects, darting past rows of trees as he attempts to lose whatever is chasing him.

Suddenly, he goes as still as a statue and slowly begins to rise. Mary screams. Quincy is shouting something. I can't move. Can't think. Up, up, up Duke goes. He's suspended in the air about ten feet above us.

A zap of electricity crackles around us. The hairs on the back of my neck stand up. My ears are ringing, my body is vibrating painfully. A blast of power knocks me to my knees. I'm vaguely aware of the others going down, too.

As I struggle to catch my breath, this . . . fireball of fear? It hits me in the stomach. Heat and fear swirl inside me; an internal terror twister.

An eerie tune plays. It's the melody of Zee's chant. At first it's faint, growing louder as each second ticks away. Still on my hands and knees, I try to lift my head but it's too heavy. Out the corner of my eye, I see Nia in the same position.

"Justin."

The sound of my name from that growly voice turns my heart to stone. I feel pressure under my chin. It's being forced up, until I'm staring at Duke. His arms and legs are spread wide as he hangs like a puppet on invisible strings.

One by one, red eyes appear in the sky around him.

25

The Seeker.

"Run and hide. I'll seek and play. Not much more time before I get my way. No one can stop me; I'll get the right number. Your world will be mine, I'll escape from my slumber."

"Let. Us. Go." I force the words through my clenched teeth.

"It all worked out so much better than I expected. Not one, not two, but I got you all. *He should have never betrayed me."*

"What . . . I don't . . ."

The face in the dark blob pulsates as the monster cackles. *"Your cries of pain, I love to hear. The more you hurt, the better the fear."*

It releases me suddenly. My head falls forward, my chin hitting my chest.

Emotions swirl through me, making me nauseous. There's anger, pain, fear. I know those are mine, but there's something else. Excitement. It's coming from the Seeker. It's enjoying this.

Duke whimpers. His body twitches as he struggles to get free.

"The games began, you were the first. Not much longer until I unleash my worst," it says. *"You're all my children, but he's my favorite one. From beginning to end, he gets to experience the fun."*

Duke plummets, landing with a thud in the thick grass. He groans in pain, clutching his side.

Anger rips through me. Every ounce of bitterness and despair bubbles to the surface.

"We're coming for you," I say between gasping breaths.

It cackles. *"I'll be waiting."*

The red eyes disappear one by one. The spooky melody fades away as darkness recedes, leaving behind a gray sky and misty fog. I clutch my chest. The only reason I know my heart is still there is because it's pounding at a dangerous rate.

We lay there for a long moment. No one speaks. There's only whimpering and ragged breathing. I shove my hands into my pocket to grab the puzzle piece. I grasp it so hard it bends.

"Is it over?" Nia asks. She moves as if to touch me, but I hold up my hand to stop her.

"Don't."

She bites her lips and nods. Her eyes are bright with tears as she hugs her knees. I force myself to sit up and touch my aching jaw. There has to be a bruise from the Seeker's punishing grip.

Mary stares off in the distance, her eyes vacant. There's no life in them.

Quincy's head is pressed against his backpack as he sways back and forth.

The air is heavy around us. Thick with pain and sadness. I exhale a shaky breath and rub my chest. It aches.

"That . . . that was horrifying," Lyric says. "What did it want?"

"Me," Duke says weakly. He shakily sits up, wincing in pain. "It likes to torment everyone, but with me it's different; there's more." His unfocused eyes stare off in the distance. "Maybe it's because I've been here so long, or because I have so many fears within me . . . There's this horrifying connection. I can't escape it no matter how far I run, no matter where I hide."

Nia wipes tears from her cheeks. "You're not alone anymore." She glances between Mary and Duke. "You don't have to fight the Seeker by yourself."

He scoffs. "Even when we're together, I'm alone."

Lyric runs a hand through his hair. "No matter how much you try to explain what you've gone through, we'll never get it. We can't. It's personal. You've *lived* it." He glances at me and Nia. "But we're here now. And like I said before, we look out for each other. We fight for each other. And we're gonna fight for you, too. It's not you against the Seeker anymore. It's *us*."

Mary's eyes flutter closed. "Us," she says wistfully.

Duke watches me. His expression is clouded with fear, but there's also a glimmer of hope. I concentrate on that.

I wearily climb to my feet and reach for my backpack. "Let's go."

Everyone stares at me, not moving.

"What? Nothing's changed." I glance from person to person. "We find Shae and Carla. We figure out a way home before the Seeker takes kid number four hundred. The plan is the same. What just happened was bad, but we knew taking down the monster wasn't going to be easy."

Lyric slowly stands. "Yeah, but I'm still shook. Can't we take five to regroup?"

"There's no time." If I think about it too much I might not be able to do what we need to do.

"He's right. I'm about as far from okay as you can get, but I'm ready to do whatever it takes to get home." Nia stands and stretches. Her bones crack. She winces.

"You okay?" I ask.

"Yeah, just . . . really stiff," she mumbles, then smiles weakly. "Did you know courage is doing stuff when you're afraid?"

I swallow hard. "Then there's no one more courageous than us."

"Truth," says Lyric.

Nia smiles. "Let's go save the world."

"After we find Carla and Shae," Quincy says as he scrambles to his feet.

Mary and Duke don't respond, but they stand and join us as we start walking again.

We solemnly continue toward the park. As we enter the gates, I stop abruptly. A group of kids, maybe fifty. They watch us with wide eyes.

"I'll say this one more time. I'm looking for my brother. His name is Quin-cy!" a raspy voice I recognize says.

"Carla!" Quincy races forward.

The crowd parts and Carla gawks at us. She lets out a wheezing gasp. "Quincy?" She touches her chest and takes an unsteady step forward. Quincy slams into her and they stumble back.

Kids scatter and yell out reminders about not touching, but it's too late and I don't think Quincy and Carla care. Their embrace is long and tight.

Quincy releases her. "Are you okay?"

Carla doubles over, her hands on her knees. "I . . . I . . . I need . . ." She wheezes.

"What's wrong with her?" Lyric asks as we hurry closer.

Quincy tugs off his backpack and quickly unzips one of the pockets. He removes an inhaler and shoves it into Carla's hand.

"She has asthma?" Nia asks.

Carla shakes the device, then brings it to her mouth. She breathes in deeply, then presses the top of the canister. She removes it and holds her breath.

"Better now?" Quincy asks.

She inhales and exhales a few breaths, then nods. "What happened to your face?"

He winces. "Bugs. They bit and stung me. What did the Seeker do to you?"

She shudders. "I . . ." She falls silent when she catches sight of our group. She stands up taller, jerking her shoulders back. "What are they doing here?"

Quincy points in our direction. "They helped me find you."

"We're glad you're okay," Nia says.

Carla snorts. "Of course I'm okay. Duh. I know how to take care of myself."

There's not as much bite to her words as usual. Her hair is tangled and there are scratches all over her face and neck.

"You better be happy my brother is safe," Carla says. "I bet all of you are to blame for whatever's happening. Fix it."

I ignore her; my gaze is locked on someone standing just behind the crowd of kids. Shae. She's dressed in one of those ballet dance outfits—a black leotard thingy with a pink, frilly skirt and tights.

"Shae!" Quincy cries happily.

I point at her. "Uh, is she real or fake?"

"Fake? What are you talking about?" Carla asks.

“Long story,” says Lyric, then he turns to Shae. “Do you have a number on your wrist?”

She slowly approaches, staring at us with wide eyes. She extends her arm. Three hundred and ninety-four.

“How did you get here?” I ask.

“I was at my dance camp, then I was here,” she says shakily. “I don’t know what happened. What kind of place is this? It’s scary.”

I glance at Lyric and Nia. The real Shae did disappear from dance camp, and she has a number.

“I want to go home.” Shae flips her long brown hair over her shoulder. “I’m sure my parents have offered a huge reward for my return. I was probably on television. I hope they used a good picture.”

Lyric rolls his eyes. “That’s definitely something the real Shae would say.”

“I’m glad you’re okay,” Quincy says to her. “I was worried about you. Not as much as I was worried about my sister, but I did think about you all the time.”

Shae looks Quincy up and down, her nose scrunched in a frown. “Uh, thanks.”

Carla shoves her inhaler in the front pocket of her baggy jeans. “I want to know what’s up with this crazy place. How do we get home?”

The murmuring around us grows louder. The kids gathered near the tree fort stare at us. My gaze darts around the group—all shapes and sizes, different races, older, younger. A surge of panic shoots through my veins as I take in some of the clothing—bell-bottom pants, tie-dyed shirts, poodle skirts, platform shoes, knee socks, leather vests with tassels. Some of these kids were taken a long time ago like Duke.

"I thought you said kids don't usually hang out together," I say to him.

His eyes twitch. "I've never seen so many together at once."

"I ran into some of them as I was walking around trying to figure out what's going on," Carla explains. "I told them I was going to find a way home and they started following me. What's this about a monster snatching us? And why is all this scary stuff happening?"

"I wasn't following you," a girl with long red hair says. She's wearing blue shorts and a green tank top. "The monster . . . the monster was chasing me and I was trying to hide."

"Me too," says a boy with a large gap in his top front teeth. He's short, with curly brown hair.

My gaze bounces between the two of them. They look familiar. How do I know them? My eyes widen. "AnnaBelle? Cameron?"

They gasp.

"How do you know my name?" she asks.

"The missing wall," I say.

"Whoa." Lyric gawks at them. "You're right."

"What's a missing wall?" AnnaBelle asks.

Nia side-eyes Mary. "We found a wall with pictures of missing kids. Your photos were up there with some of our friends."

"Was I on the news?" Cameron asks. "Are my mom and dad looking for me?"

"Yeah, man. I'm sure they are," Lyric says.

I glance at Cameron's wrists, then AnnaBelle's. He's number 325. AnnaBelle is 307.

"Do you really know a way home?" a small boy in superhero pajamas asks. His chubby face is pale and his eyes are red from crying.

The other kids begin to shout questions.

Duke turns away, his shoulders hunched.

"Is that him?" a girl whispers to the kids around her as she stares at Duke.

"Maybe. I think so," a boy responds. "So, he is real? They say he's been here forever."

"What's wrong with him?" another boy asks.

Duke tugs at the collar of his shirt, muttering to himself. His wide eyes dart around. "Out in the open. Not a good idea."

"Duke." I step closer to him.

Flinching, he shuffles back. "Too close."

I stop. "Sorry." I realize this is probably the first time he's been around this many people in a very long time. And we're even farther away from his woods. His safe place. This is clearly hard on him.

"We should tell them what we know," he says. "Tell them so we can go."

I nod. "Let's go to the amphitheater. We can—"

"Justin," Not-Mom's voice whispers. "I'm coming for you. We'll be a family again."

I spin around, my eyes searching the area. She stands in the shadow of a large tree.

"Justin," she whispers again. My skin crawls.

Mary sucks in a loud breath. I touched her. She can see Not-Mom.

"What is it?" asks Nia.

"No one," I say. "I mean, it's nothing."

Nia frowns, but before she can ask me anything else, I quickly walk over to the amphitheater.

I jump onto the small stage as the kids settle on the concrete stairs arranged in a half circle. Nia, Lyric, Mary, and Duke join me. I count the kids. Forty-five. That's a small number considering there are almost four hundred in Nowhere.

Soft murmurs and faint crying drift past me as kids stare fearfully in our direction. I slide my backpack off my shoulders as if that will lighten the heavy responsibility I feel.

"Well, talk already." Carla sits in the front row.

I glance at Duke. He gestures for me to speak. I thought for sure he'd want to explain everything since he's been here longer than me.

I clear my throat. "My name is Justin."

The silence is thick as I gaze at the scared faces before me. I slide my hand into my pocket and grasp the puzzle piece. Where to start?

I hold up my arm, deciding to focus on what's most important at the moment. "The number on your wrist, we all have them. We figured out that the Seeker is keeping track of the number of kids in Nowhere."

I watch as kids glance down at the wrists, touching the marks. "I'm number 399."

"We don't want it to reach four hundred," Lyric says.

"Why?" Carla asks with a frown.

I swallow hard. "We believe if the monster reaches that number, it'll be able to leave this place and enter our world for good. All the fears and scary stuff—"

"No kid will be safe," Nia says.

The boy wearing the pajamas whimpers. "So, the monster could take my brother and sister, too?"

"Not if we stop it," Mary says.

"I want to go home," a kid cries.

"Why did it bring me to this place? I want my mom," says AnnaBelle.

"How do we leave?"

It's rapid-fire questions and comments. The level of the frantic voices rises until it's almost painful.

Finally, Duke whistles so loudly I flinch. "Too much noise. They'll hear you. They'll come and it will be bad. Very bad."

Instantly, there's quiet. Kids stare wide-eyed at Duke.

"Listen, I know this is hard to hear. It was scary for us, too, but we found out that the monster takes kids who break the rules of Hide and Seek," I explain.

"What?" cries Shae. "A man with a scar came to camp and passed out ice cream."

Mary gasps.

"He saw us playing games and started going on and on about Hide and Seek," Shae explains. "Me and my friends decided to play it, but then I got hot and didn't want to sweat so I quit."

"Dude!" cries Lyric. "He set her up, too."

"I don't understand," says Carla. "You're saying we're here because of a stupid game?"

"The Seeker's game." Duke sways back and forth. "You played, you pay."

"Long story short . . . we found out the monster was going to snatch us and bring us here," I say.

Nia steps forward. "Since we had that information, we tried to come up with a plan to help us escape once we arrived."

Lyric shrugs off his backpack and holds it up. "We saw Quincy get taken while wearing one of these, so we decided to sneak in supplies to fight the Seeker. It worked."

Quincy perks up and puffs out his chest.

"Estas enojando el monstruo," a boy yells out. "Es peor para nosotros ahora."

I frown. "What did he say? I don't know Spanish."

Shae jumps up. "I do, I do, I do. I have a tutor."

Carla rolls her eyes.

"He said, 'You're making the monster mad' and 'It's worse for us now.'"

A fierce wind whips past us. It howls and bolts of lightning slash through the darkening sky.

"The monster is stronger because it's almost achieved its goal to capture four hundred kids," Duke says, raising his voice to compete with the wind. "We have to stop it."

"How did you figure this all out?" Carla says, her forehead creased.

"Zee. Remember those weird chants?" Lyric asks. "He was trying to warn us."

Carla face-palms. "Are you kiddin' me? We're listening to him?"

Nia leans close and whispers, "You need to tell them everything."

Grimacing, I nod. They should know what will happen once we get home.

"There's more." I wish all the kids were here. It's not fair they have no idea what is going on. This will affect them, too.

"Well?" Carla says, throwing her hands up in frustration. "What is it?"

"You age," I blurt out. "Time stops here, but when you leave all those years catch up to you."

26

"You age? So? I don't get it," Carla says.

Lyric groans. "Think about it."

"I understand," Shae says, twirling a long piece of her hair. "Some of these kids are gonna be super old when they leave."

Carla's eyes widen. Her gaze jumps around, taking in the faces of the kids. "Oh. I—"

"Wait, wait, wait." Duke shakes his head. "We age? I've been gone eighty years and I was thirteen when the Seeker took me. You're saying if we return, I'll be ninety-three? I won't be thirteen anymore?"

"Yeah," Lyric says.

Duke stumbles back and doubles over. His hands rest on his knees. "I'll be . . . I could . . ."

My wide eyes bounce between Mary and Duke. "You didn't know?"

"No." His voice cracks as he slowly lifts his head. He turns to Mary. "Did you?"

She winces and lowers her eyes.

Duke's devastated expression morphs into anger. "You knew?" he asks sharply.

"Yeah." She twists the bottom of her dingy shirt. "I'm . . . I'm sorry. We talked about going home, but I didn't think we'd ever get out so it didn't matter."

Duke gawks at her. "*It didn't matter?*"

Nia twists her braids into knots. "I don't get it. We have a plan. You agreed to help us."

"Mary, what else didn't matter?" I ask with growing dread. "What else didn't you tell Duke?"

She flinches. "I . . ."

"Oh man. I sense some major betrayal." Lyric runs a hand down his face. "You know about her brother, Hyde, right?" he asks Duke. "He was here, too, but he decided to work with the Seeker. It let him out to trick kids into playing the game. He sold us out."

Duke clutches his head. "Why . . . All this time . . ."

Suddenly, something the Seeker said pops into my mind. *The games began, you were the first. Not much longer until I'll unleash my worst.*

I slowly approach Duke. "What number are you?"

He tugs back a long sleeve and extends his arm so I can see his mark.

One.

I tremble. Nia and Lyric suck in a loud breath. In the woods I saw the number one, but thought it was for one hundred and something. But he was the first kid the Seeker stole.

"The Seeker really has taken everything from me," Duke whispers, staggering a few feet away.

He'll be ninety-three. What if he goes through all this, fights the Seeker, and dies the moment we reach home? My hands curl into fists. I want to howl my anger. It's not fair!

"I'll be twenty-two," a girl cries.

"Thirty-seven."

A chorus of voices erupt like a volcano. Anger and confusion flow through the amphitheater like lava, echoing through the park.

"Forty-nine."

"Sixty-two."

Kids call out ages as they calculate the math.

"At least you'll be home. Anything is better than Nowhere, right?" Shae asks.

"Easy for y'all to say," says a thin boy with long shaggy hair. He's wearing dirty overalls. "I'll be almost fifty."

I was so focused on escaping as fast as possible, I never considered how it would affect all the other Nowhere kids. Zee was gone a little over a year so not much changed. But for Duke and some others—it's a lifetime.

"What did y'all expect to happen?" Carla asks. "That you'd go back and still be a kid? That the world would rewind or something?" She seems honestly confused.

"What if we don't leave?" a boy with long, dark hair says. He's wearing knee-length shorts, sandals, and a worn T-shirt with a picture of ocean waves and a surf board across the front. "I'll be seventy-eight. My family . . . what if they're not around anymore?"

"We could help each other," Nia says shakily.

"How? You'll still be a kid. I'll be old."

Nia flinches.

"You'd rather stay lost and scared?" Lyric asks, shaking his head as if the thought is unimaginable.

The surfer kid turns away. His chin trembles.

Duke pins Mary with a hard glare. "You should have told me *everything*."

"I'm sorry," she whispers, wiping tears from her eyes.

He turns to me. "We destroy the Seeker. Whatever happens after that—" His jaw clenches. "I'm in no matter what."

Kids yell out their agreement or voice their despair. Some slip away.

"Man, this is messed up." Lyric runs his fingers through his tangled hair. “Think about all those other kids in Nowhere. They have no idea what will happen to them when they return home.”

“There’s nothing we can do,” I say. “It’s not like we can find them all and fill them in.”

“Are we done with all this talkin’?” asks Carla. “How do we get home?”

I run a hand down my face. “That’s what we need to—”

There’s a loud rumble and the ground shakes. The concrete bleachers split; kids tumble to the ground.

“Whoa.” The stage tilts at a steep angle. Flailing around, we slide to the ground. I roll away from the debris of cracked stones.

Screaming, kids scramble out of the crumbling amphitheater and attempt to flee in different directions. Desperate to escape, they bump into each other and their cries of horror echo around us.

“What the—” I watch as an invisible force lifts the surfer kid up toward the sky as he runs away. He bobs up and down, and sputters as if he’s underwater.

“What is it? What’s happening?” Quincy cries.

“Ooomph.” Duke staggers back, clutching his stomach. “They’re here.” His head jerks back as if someone has delivered an uppercut to his chin. He hits the ground with a thud.

Nia tugs on my backpack. “What are we gonna do?”

“Justin! Nia!” Lyric glances around frantically. “Where are you?”

“Here,” Nia says, moving to stand right in front of him.

"They're beside you," Mary tells Lyric.

Panting, he swings in our direction. His gaze is a little off to the right. "Don't leave me," he pleads.

My mind is spinning quickly, but it's like the action in front of me is happening in slow motion. The volume of the noise rises and falls.

"Get them off!" AnnaBelle rolls around, screaming in pain. "Get them off!"

Quincy rushes toward her, but Duke crawls to his feet and jumps into his path, blocking him. "Don't touch her."

"But, but . . . we have to help," Quincy says. The ground under our feet shifts and rolls like ocean waves. A giant hole appears. AnnaBelle, a few inches off the ground, speeds toward the large opening as if she's being carried. She disappears within the pit.

All around me kids are being attacked by their fears. It doesn't matter that I can't see what they see; I feel connected to them. Like the terror is traveling, searching for the next person to torture.

"What are we doing?" Carla asks. "Somebody make a decision."

"We can't stay here," Shae cries.

Breathe. Must breathe. It's chaos all around us.

"Justin! Nia!" Lyric calls out.

I reach for him, but my hand drops to my side. Can't touch him.

"Follow me," Mary tells Lyric. "I won't let you lose them."

We run. And run. And run. We race out of the park and down

the street with no specific destination in mind. We're followed by screams and cries for help.

Adrenaline has me moving much faster than I ever imagined running in my life. Finally, out of breath, I collapse in the middle of the baseball field near our school. Bodies fall around me. Nia, Lyric, Carla, Quincy, Shae, Duke, Mary.

27

All those kids back there . . .

My heart is racing. Black dots swim across my eyes. One. Two. Three. Four. Breathe. Sweat trickles down the side of my face. Breathe. Inhale. Exhale.

"We had to leave them," Duke mumbles to himself as if he's reading my mind. "There was nothing we could do."

"Justin?" Nia says.

I squeeze my eyes shut. One. Two. Three. Four. Breathe.

"Are you okay?" she asks.

The truth is no. A very big no, but I can't make myself say it out loud. I reach for my pocket. It's enough just to rest my hand there, feeling the outline of the puzzle piece. Breathe. Count. Breathe. The spike of adrenaline I felt during our escape from the park plummets, leaving me weak and shaky. I'm tired. So tired.

The silence around me is painful, prickling my skin. Everyone is slumped over, gasping for air. Their clothes and hair are disheveled. The expressions are the same—terror and confusion.

My eyes lock on Lyric.

His face is flushed. There's a scar across his cheek. I'm not sure when it happened. Maybe during the madness in the park.

He smiles weakly.

"You can see me now?" I ask.

He swallows hard. "Yeah, but I can't always."

Nia scoots close to him. "When I first found you here, I was calling your name, but you didn't know I was there, did you?"

Lyric looks away, unable to meet her eyes. "No."

"That's why you ran. You didn't hear me. Then we found Justin and . . ." She frowns. "And . . ." She frowns.

When she doesn't continue, I ask, "What?"

"I forgot what I was going to say."

I watch her closely. She fidgets with the buttons on her shirt. "It was nothing."

"It's always something," Duke says with a heavy sigh. "Always."

Shae hugs herself. "I'm scared."

"What are we gonna do now?" Carla uses her inhaler, then shoves it back in her pocket.

"We stick to the plan," says Duke. "We stop the Seeker."

"Do we really have to fight a monster?" Shae asks. "There's no other way to get home?"

"I'll protect you," Quincy says.

Shae rolls her eyes.

There's a loud grumble. I jump and my gaze whips around.

"That's my stomach. I'm hungry." Carla tugs on Lyric's backpack with him still attached. "You got some food in there?"

"Hey, watch it." He leans away. "Your brother has a backpack, too."

"Carla, I brought all your favorite snacks." Quincy unzips a pocket. He hands her a pouch of cinnamon applesauce, a fruit cup, and a string cheese.

She blushes, but takes the food.

"Uh, I'm not sure that cheese is safe. Two days without refrigeration sounds dangerous to me," says Lyric.

Carla squeezes the applesauce packet in her mouth and mumbles something I can't make out.

I guess we're taking a snack break. Regrouping. That's fine with me.

"I have some stuff, too." I pass out some packaged cookies. Lyric packed some peanuts and chocolate. He passes those treats around.

Mary gazes longingly at the cookies.

"Wait, do you eat?" I don't know much about the basic day-to-day stuff.

"When I first arrived, I was hungry." Duke runs his hand over the scar on his head.

"After a while, you lose your appetite," Mary says.

"That sucks." Carla peels opens the fruit cup and drinks the syrup.

I wait for Nia to burst out a fun fact about food or digestion, but she remains silent. She tugs on some long blades of grass, her expression blank.

Quincy shoves several cookies in his mouth. His cheeks bulge as he chews. Crumbs coat his smacking lips.

Duke stares at a candy bar for a long moment. He unwraps it, then hesitantly takes a bite. His eyes immediately light up. "I forgot how much I like chocolate," he says quietly.

He takes another big bite.

"Careful," says Lyric. "You'll probably get a serious sugar rush."

"I'm already feeling it," Duke says with a smile.

It's the first time I've ever seen a happy expression on his face. He looks different. Lighter.

"It's like a burst of energy," he says. "I haven't felt this since . . ." His smile slips away and the haunted expression returns.

Mary nibbles on a cookie. Some color seeps into her pale face. Maybe she's getting the boost like Duke. Maybe it'll give them extra strength to deal with the Seeker.

I dust salt and dirt off my hands with a wipe from my backpack. I shift left and right, stretching my sore, bruised limbs. For a moment, I let myself pretend I'm eating lunch with my friends at school, and there's not something ready to jump out and scare us at any moment. The crackling of the wrappers and sounds of chewing are comforting. I have to enjoy this because I know it won't last long.

Carla finishes her fruit cup. "We can't sit here forever. What's next? How do we get back home?"

See. Didn't even get five minutes of peace.

"We have to go through the Seeker," Duke says. "It knows we're coming and it's getting ready for us."

"How do you know?" Mary asks.

Duke rubs his chest, but doesn't respond to her question.

She sighs and turns away. Is he not talking to her now? This is going to be a problem. We have to work together.

"How do we fight the Seeker?" Quincy asks. "It's so strong and scary."

"Some of our supplies helped with the fear attacks. Maybe we can use other stuff we brought against the monster," I say.

Lyric and I dump out our backpacks. There's a pile of odd items.

"Glow sticks?" asks Shae. "I used these in one of my dance routines. I was awesome."

"Looks like a bunch of junk to me," Carla says. "How's Silly String, a slingshot, rope, a whistle, a Swiss Army knife, and all that other crazy stuff supposed to take down a monster?"

Duke grabs a flashlight and switches it on and off. “Pepper spray saved Mary.”

Mary snorts. “Glad something helped, since you didn’t.”

I sigh. Okay, here we go.

“Someone is bit-ter,” Shae mumbles.

“You know why I couldn’t help,” Duke says through gritted teeth.

Mary waves off his response. “It doesn’t matter now. You made a decision *not* to take on my fear, so you should understand why I made a decision *not* to tell you about my brother and stuff.”

“Drama,” Shae whispers as she chews on a cookie. Her wide eyes are fixed on Mary and Duke like she’s watching a movie play out before her.

“Stuff?! You call aging to the point of possible death ‘stuff’?” Duke asks. “Me knowing about your rat snake fear doesn’t compare to all the secrets you kept.”

Lyric leans close to me and whispers, “Mommy and Daddy are fighting. Make it stop.”

Shae scoots closer, wiping crumbs off her face. “Rat snakes? Are we sharing our feelings and talking about our fears? I’m scared of dolls.”

My head whips around to her. What is happening right now? I’m so confused.

“Dolls?” asks Nia.

Shae nods. “My mom collected them as a kid and thinks I should like them, too. She puts them all over my bedroom. At night, I sleep with the covers over my head so I don't have to see them staring at me with their creepy marble eyes."

"What do the dolls do to you here?" I ask.

Shae shudders. "They're alive and they want to play with me. It's horrible." She turns to Carla. "What about you?"

"Girl, please." Carla snorts. "I'm not tellin' y'all nothing. My stuff is personal."

My eyes close briefly. Dread crawls through me. This is actually a conversation we need to have. We probably should have had it earlier.

I massage the back of my neck. "Look, this is not . . . I don't want to talk about my fear either, but we have a better chance of surviving and winning if we know everyone's fears. When they appear, we can help each other."

There is a moment of hesitation as we all look around. The silence is uncomfortable. We're a strange group. Only Lyric and Nia are my close friends, and even they don't know all the personal stuff I deal with. Now I have to share my fears with *everyone,* for the greater good.

Carla grumbles.

Lyric sighs heavily. "What happens in Nowhere stays in Nowhere, right?"

We all nod in agreement. Rain trickles from the clouds. It's like the sky is weeping for us.

"And don't be judgy." Nia directs that to Carla.

"Whatever," she says with an eye roll.

"You already heard I'm scared of rats and snakes," Mary says. "It's the worst of both animals combined."

Carla gawks at her.

Shae holds up her hand, like she's in class and wants the teacher to call on her.

"Yes, Shae?" Quincy says with a huge smile.

"I didn't tell you everything. Not that it's a competition, but I want you to know my fear is just as scary as Mary's. The dolls are the weird antique kind with the porcelain heads and yarn hair. When they touch you, you turn into one."

"Whaaaaat?" says Lyric.

"That *is* scary," says Quincy.

Shae twirls a lock of her hair. "I know, right?"

Carla rolls her eyes.

"I'll go next," says Quincy. "I'm scared of bugs." He gestures at his face. "They bite and sting. It hurts bad." He turns to Lyric, who sits next to him. "You next."

A muscle ticks in Lyric's jaw. "It's . . . it's being alone, no it's more like . . ." He glances at me and Nia. "My family is questionable, but I've always been able to count on y'all. You always have my back. You're always there for me. My fear is not having you around, especially when I need you the most. During my fears, I can't see you or find you."

Nia's chin trembles. "We're always here. Even when you don't see us."

Lyric pushes his hair off his forehead. "Yeah, but it's also that I know you're in trouble and I can't get to you. I'm useless."

I've always known our friendship was special, but Lyric's words hit me hard. I open my mouth to respond, but he shakes his head.

"You know how I feel about big emotional moments." He fake shudders. "Let's move on."

"I'll go." Duke rubs his palms over his thin pants. "Besides the Seeker, I'm afraid of lots of things because of all the kids I've touched. Eleven fears total. I think it's eleven. Fire, dogs, heights, the dark, lightning, crows, flying, dentists, shadows—"

"Shadows? Who's afraid of a shadow?" Carla asks.

"One boy I met was apparently afraid of his own shadow." Duke swipes at the sweat trickling down his cheek. "It would come alive and attack him."

"Is that what attacked you in the amphitheater?" I saw him take a punch, double over, and fall.

"Yeah," he says.

Lyric shakes his head in disbelief. "Man, that takes shadow boxing to another level."

"Spiderwebs scare me the most, though," Duke says. "I hate that you don't see them until it's too late and then they stick to you. Here, the webs wrap me up in a human cocoon. It's dark, hard to breathe . . . I'm trapped and spiders crawl all over me."

"Daaaaang," says Lyric.

Out of all the fears Duke mentioned, I wonder if dying is now his biggest. I want to ask him how he feels about everything, but it seems wrong to question him about it. If I'm having a hard time imagining what will happen, it has to be a hundred times worse for him.

As if he feels my eyes on him, he glances in my direction. Sadness and determination shine bright.

Carla crosses her arms and mumbles something.

"What?" asks Mary.

She huffs. "Myself. That's my fear. I see myself, but different, okay? I'm not nice."

"Wait. I don't get it," says Lyric. "You're not nice now. How is that a fear?"

She glares at him. "*I am* nice, just not to you. And I have friends. People like me. The other me is really mean. I'm not that person."

Nia rubs her temples. "So, you're afraid of not being liked, being a meaner version of yourself?"

"Say something about it and I'll beat your face in," says Carla.

Lyric's jaw drops. "Whoa, meaner than this? Yeah, okay. That's terrifying."

"Next!" Carla says.

Nia hugs her knees. "My fear is forgetting stuff like my grandma."

Nia's head is filled with a lot of information and those facts give her confidence since she's not so good with regular schoolwork. Forgetting stuff, not knowing . . . I understand how that is scary to her.

I lean close, so only she can hear me. "All you need to remember is that you're one of my best friends. We got this."

"So, what about you?" Carla asks me. "You haven't said."

I chew on the inside of my cheek as I try to get the words out. Mary knows. She saw.

"It's my mom. When she was sick and, uh, died."

"Dude . . ." Lyric says.

I stare at the ground. I feel everyone's eyes on me.

"You see your dead mom?" asks Carla.

"It's the worst and scariest version of her," I whisper.

"I'm sorry, Justin," says Nia.

There's a long moment of awkward silence.

Carla tosses her trash over her shoulder. "Okay, so we know what everyone is afraid of."

My head pops up. No snide comment or insults?

She grabs her inhaler and gives it a hard shake before inhaling deeply. "What now?" she asks, her eyes surprisingly sympathetic. "I'm getting the feeling y'all don't know what to do next."

"Someone might," I say carefully.

"Who?" asks Mary. "My brother wouldn't—"

"Not him. Zee," I say.

Carla groans. "We're done for."

"Hyde sensed that we were around even though he couldn't see us," I say.

Lyric nods. "I see where you're going with this. Maybe Zee would know we are there and help us somehow like he did before."

"He could tell us something that will help destroy the monster," Nia says.

I climb to my feet, suddenly anxious to see Zee.

"And if he can't or won't help?" asks Mary with a weary sigh.

"We'll lose and the Seeker will win?" Quincy asks.

"Never that," says Lyric. "Zee will help us. I'm sure of it. Then we'll have a plan to get some payback." He rubs his palms together. "Time for Mission Seek and Destroy the Seeker."

Duke's hands ball into fists. "Game on."

28

I stand in a familiar spot—on the sidewalk in front of Zee's house. The sky is filled with fat, gray clouds, just like everywhere else in Nowhere. Streaks of dirt cover all the windows, making it impossible to peek in. The welcome home decorations—wilted blue balloons and torn crinkled streamers—are a reminder of what went so wrong.

Zee came back changed from this place.

"I just got hit with a scary sense of déjà vu," says Nia.

How will the memories of Nowhere affect us?

"Dude." That's all Lyric says, but the one word is more than a thousand. He understands how big this moment is.

"Are we going in or what?" asks Carla. "Y'all are moving slowwwwww."

"And it's creepy out here," says Quincy.

He's not lying. It's dark, but not completely and the air crackles with this strange vibe that puts me on edge. The lights from within Zee's house cast an eerie glow that only adds to the spookiness.

Breathe. It should be automatic, but I keep forgetting how to. The lack of oxygen to my brain is making me shaky.

"We should—"

Duke is interrupted by the sound of bells ringing. Startled, I turn and see two little girls, on pink bikes, riding toward us. They're wearing black princess dresses with lots of lace and bows.

"Is anyone else seeing this?" Lyric says, his voice low. "Or am I losin' it?"

"I see them," Nia says. Her voice shakes.

I blink rapidly, hoping it's just my imagination. The girls have elongated heads and eyes the size of baseballs. Their skin is gray with dark veins clearly visible, like spider webs, all over their face. They smirk as they draw near.

In high-pitched cheery voices, the girls chant, "The Seeker is coming! The Seeker is coming! Four hundred is its final number to wake it from its prison of slumber."

The hairs on my arms lift. We all shuffle back onto Zee's front lawn.

"What, the nightmare is happening now?" Lyric asks with wide eyes.

The girls giggle as they ride past us and continue to chant, "The Seeker is coming! The Seeker is coming! There's nowhere safe, get ready to run. The Seeker is about to have some fun!"

Quincy covers his ears with his hands.

We watch as they reach the end of the block. A shimmering light appears. It pulsates like a beating heart. The creepy girls peek over their shoulders, giggle, then disappear inside the bright vortex.

"Where'd they go?" Shae cries.

Duke spins toward me. "You say your friend can help. Well, we need to find out if you're right. Now!"

I gulp and glance at Zee's house. "Okay. Let's go, but not through the front." I don't want to walk inside like that. It feels wrong. Shifting my backpack on my shoulders, I circle the house and we enter through the backyard fence. I stop abruptly, causing a traffic jam.

Zee stands on the back porch. It's almost as if he was waiting for us to arrive. He hits his head with his fist. "My fault. Sorry. My fault. All alone. Couldn't stay. The falling. So high. Kept falling," Zee mutters.

Carla sighs. "Yep. We're done for."

"What's Zee talking about?" asks Quincy as we file inside the backyard.

"Look, he's holding the harmonica that I gave him," Lyric whispers.

I rub my chest, but it doesn't ease the pain. Zee seems worse than when we left him.

"Didn't mean it. Didn't mean it," Zee says. His voice cracks. "Had to take it. Had to leave. So scared. Always falling. Sorry. So sorry."

"I don't understand. Is he apologizing for attacking us?" Nia steps around an overturned table from the party.

Maybe, but with everything that's gone down, I'm not so sure now. My legs tremble as I move closer.

"Falling?" I swallow hard. Once when we were riding a roller coaster, Zee's safety bar didn't lock all the way. He almost fell off the ride. He's been super afraid of heights and roller coasters ever since. Is that what he experienced in Nowhere?

"Couldn't do it. Couldn't do it." Zee paces back and forth along the porch, clutching his head. "Best friends. No deal. No deal."

"Why is he acting like this?" asks Shae.

Mary watches Zee closely. "He has that look in his eyes. The same one my brother had."

"Some bad stuff must have happened to him," Carla says, as if she now understands Zee a little better.

"It's guilt," Mary says. "My brother was off for a while, too, but then he got over it. Zee hasn't."

"Hold up. What are you saying?" Lyric's eyes flash a warning.

That seed of uncertainty inside me sprouts, planting deep, painful roots.

Nia shakes her head. "Zee *is not* like Hyde."

"Are you sure?" Mary asks. "No one escapes Nowhere."

"Wait. You think he . . . ?" Lyric shakes his head. "No, no way! He'd never do that."

"What are you talking about?" Shae asks, her head whipping back and forth between us.

I reach into my pocket and hold the puzzle piece tight. "Mary thinks Zee betrayed us. That the Seeker sent him back to trick us like Hyde. She . . . she believes he took a deal, like her brother."

"Well, she's wrong." Lyric's nostrils flare as he glares at her. "He's innocent."

"He . . . he wouldn't . . ." Nia's bright eyes plead with me to agree.

I turn away, unable to look at Zee. My heart seizes and I struggle to catch my breath. Inhale. Exhale. The air is thin. I feel light-headed.

Lyric growls. "We can trust him! He's our friend. He warned us."

He did. He did warn us, but . . .

"I didn't wanna believe my brother could betray me either," Mary says. "But he did." She turns to Duke. "I didn't tell you because I was scared you would think I could be like him and you wouldn't help me."

Duke stares at her for a moment, then shakes his head. "The truth. I deserved the truth."

There hasn't been much I can count on in the past couple of years, but no matter what happened, even when things were the worst, I had Zee. I believed in Zee.

"It came because of me. Because of me," he mumbles. "My fault."

I exhale a shaky breath. Is Zee saying the Seeker targeted us because he backed out of the deal? The Seeker wanted revenge? My chest tightens as I think back on everything that has happened, all of Zee's ramblings, the Seeker's taunts . . . We were its endgame all along.

"It's cold," says Shae, shivering. "Why is it so cold now?" Her breath clouds out in front of her.

"Justin, what do we do now?" Quincy asks.

I told him and everyone else that we were going home. I made them believe. Why did I do that?

Black dots. Inhale. Exhale. Breathe. I grit my teeth. Pull it together, Justin. Breathe.

"I'm leaving," Carla says, reaching for her brother. "C'mon, Quincy. We can find another way home."

"But . . . but . . ." he stutters. "The supplies. The monster—"

"You can't go," says Nia. "We have to work as a team."

Carla stares at the ground, then back at Nia. "I've never been on your team. You don't even like me."

Shae hugs herself tight. "I want to leave, too. I don't want to be here."

"Wait! We came this far. We can't give up now. I can't just go back," says Duke.

All their noise builds until I think my head will explode. I fight my way out of the bubble of doubt, fear, and confusion that has surrounded me.

"Zee," I blurt out. "Zee!" My voice is louder this time.

The noise around me stops. Everyone stares at me like I've lost my mind.

I approach him and stand at the bottom of the porch steps. "It's okay. If you were sent back to . . ." I'm out of breath, like I've been running a marathon. "You were alone and scared. I'm sorry you didn't have anyone there to help you." I blink back tears. "Even if you took the deal at first, what matters is that you didn't do what the Seeker wanted. You weren't the reason we played the game. That's not on you. And in your own way, you tried to help us. That counts more than anything else. You hear me?!"

Nia makes her way to my side. "Maybe that's why he's like this. All the pressure was too much. It broke him."

"Don't ask me to believe that," says Lyric, his eyes bright.

I rub my aching chest. "We're the Fantastic Four, right? Nothing can change that. No mistakes. No monster."

Lyric stares at Zee, who is mumbling to himself as he paces the porch.

"Zee is still Zee. He's just in pieces. We can help put him back together again." I trade glances with Lyric and Nia. "By defeating the Seeker we can make it better."

"Friends don't give up on friends." Lyric faces Zee. "And we're more than friends. We're family. Do you hear us? We're not giving up!"

Zee's gaze jerks upward at the dark sky. This blackness feels completely evil and permanent.

"Zee," Mrs. Murphy calls from inside the house. "Your lunch is ready. Come on in, sweetie."

He squeezes his eyes closed. "It all began with Hide and Seek. The rules you broke you now must keep," Zee chants. "The Seeker hides and fear's the game. To win, it must not end the same."

"He warned us before, maybe he's doing it again," says Nia.

I move closer. "Say it again, Zee."

He whimpers and tugs at his hair. We can't lose him now. His face contorts as if he's in agony. "Can't . . . can't . . ." He half turns away, then swings back around, but it's like it takes a big effort.

"Please, Zee," I say. "We need your help."

"Zee?" Mrs. Murphy yells.

His tortured expression slips off his face and an eerie calmness settles over him. He points to the tree in the middle of his backyard. "It all began with Hide and Seek. The rules you broke you now must keep. The Seeker hides and fear's the game. To win, it must not end the same."

"He's pointing to the tree we used as home base," Quincy says.

Despite the absence of light, shadows crawl and weave around the trunk of the tree. The limbs sway as if they are waving, beckoning us closer.

"Use home base to return home," Duke mutters to himself. "To end it all, we have to start at the beginning."

My head whips from the tree to Zee. I repeat his chant. I know what he's telling us to do. I draw in a loud breath.

"What is it?" asks Nia.

"I think he's saying we need to play the game again. That we have to *win* the game."

"That's how this all started," a wide-eyed Lyric says. "For everyone."

"A do-over," says Nia.

"What?" Carla steps back. "I don't wanna play that game with y'all again."

From the back porch, Zee says the chant again. Louder this time, almost screeching it.

"How do we know he's telling us the right thing to do?" Quincy clutches the straps of his backpack.

Tears stream down Zee's thin, pale face. He shouts the chant. His arm trembles as he continues to point to the tree.

I walk up to Zee and stand directly in front of him. He stops yelling mid-chant and his arm slowly lowers.

"I trust you," I say. "I believe in you. You're our friend. No matter what."

Zee's head tilts to the side. His dark eyes clear slightly. He extends his fist, off to the side. I hear Nia gasp. Tears momentarily blind me and I have to blink them away. I bite my lip, drawing blood. The pain of my heart breaking almost knocks me to my knees.

I place my hand close to his, our knuckles almost touching. He doesn't react, but I didn't expect him to. Some part of him recognizes that we're here and that's enough. Lyric and Nia jog up behind me and place their hands near Zee's as well. The Fantastic Four.

"Zee?!" Mrs. Murphy rushes out the back door and onto the porch. "Are you okay? Why didn't you answer me?" She glances around the backyard and the muscles around my heart tighten.

I take a step forward and open my mouth to . . . I'm not sure what I want to say. I wish she knew we were here and that we're fighting for Zee, fighting to get back home.

"Justin," Zee says.

My heart expands like an over-inflated balloon. Hurts.

Mrs. Murphy gently grabs his shoulders and turns him around so they face each other.

"The police are gonna find him, baby. Justin is smart, wherever he is . . ." Her voice cracks. "All your friends are coming home. I know it."

Zee lifts the harmonica to his mouth and blows out a haunting, low sound. It's off-key and sad, but uplifting as well. There's a promise in that melody, a call to action that I accept.

With her arm around Zee's shoulder, Mrs. Murphy leads him inside the house. The door slams shut behind them.

"See ya, Zee," Lyric whispers.

Soon. And he'll see us. I *promise.*

Nia waves. "Bye, Mrs. Murphy."

I clutch my puzzle piece tight, then turn to face everyone. "Let's finish this."

29

"We all lost the game. This time it's about winning, following the rules we set," I say as the wind whips up. It rattles the old patio furniture littered about the backyard.

"I don't understand." Shae shivers.

Quincy hugs himself. "Bad stuff happened last time we played Hide and Seek."

"Zee was saying we need to play the game *and win*, then we can reverse what went down," Lyric says. "We know better; we do better."

"And that's all? You think if we do this, we go home." Carla crosses her arms. "Sounds too easy."

"Don't forget we'll have our fears to deal with," says Lyric. "No way the monster is gonna go down without a fight."

"We have to be prepared for the Seeker to unleash everything it has at us," says Duke. "We're fighting for our lives, but so is the Seeker."

"I think . . ." Nia hesitates. "Hide and Seek is usually every kid for themselves, but now we're gonna have to work together and help each other make it to home base."

"Rules?" Shae rubs away the goose bumps on her arms.

I gulp. The Seeker as Shae asked the same thing when we played at Zee's house.

"If you're tagged, you're out," I say shakily. "You can't reveal the hiding place of another player. Can't hide inside a building or car. Only hide in the set backyard area. Touch home base to be safe. You can't block home base from any player. No roughing up anybody. And we have to finish the game." I focus my attention on Carla. "We play fair and honest this time. We have to."

"Don't look at me. I wasn't the only one who messed up," Carla says.

"Okay, okay. It doesn't matter now. How do we get the Seeker here?" I ask.

Duke shakes his head. "Hide and Seek is its *purpose*." He stares at the tree. "The Seeker will come. It always does. That hasn't changed in eighty years."

My eyes slowly travel around the group. Same game, with the addition of new players. And this game means so much more than the other one. Before we were playing to pass the time, now we're playing for our lives, our freedom.

I extend my arm. It trembles. "The only way to win is by helping each other. That means we need to see all of the fears. Anyone got a problem with that?" I look at Duke and Mary.

Duke pales. "All the fears at once . . ."

"You sure about this?" Mary asks.

Lyric exhales loudly. "Dude, this hand stack . . . We really will be Team Terror. All in. There's no coming back from this."

"At least we'll know what to expect," I say.

Nia bites her lip and slowly places her hand over mine. Instantly there's a shock as we share fears. Lyric tags us. His hand covers ours. After a moment of hesitation, one hand after another falls onto the pile, until we are all joined.

An energy current flows through our bodies, as we're jolted by this creepy connection. Our fingers twitch where we touch.

I point toward the large oak tree in the center of the backyard. "That'll be home base."

Stepping back, Lyric and I dump the items from our backpacks onto the ground. "Use whatever you need against the fears. Remember, *everyone* has to reach the tree. No weak attempts."

"I'm not so sure about this," says Carla. "Too much could go wrong."

Hisssss. Large black crows appear, swooping low. They land on Zee's roof.

"The crows again? Aren't they bad luck?" Lyric asks.

Duke gasps. Crows are one of his fears. He peers at the birds through narrowed eyes. "Wait, those aren't crows, they're—"

"Vultures," says Nia faintly.

"What?!" Carla says.

"Did you know vultures are scavengers? They eat dead animals." Nia frowns. "They, uh, they also attack the wounded and the sick," she says as if she is struggling to get the information out.

"Are you saying they're here to eat us?" Quincy's voice is so high the sound hurts my ears.

It's a good question, but one I wish he hadn't asked aloud. Are the birds waiting to see who remains or will they attack to prevent us from finishing the game?

The vultures hiss and their round heads bob left and right as they stare down at us with their beady eyes. I miss the crows.

A crackle of lightning zigzags through the sky. A cloud appears in the black sky, partially lit from inside. A face appears. It's so quick, I almost think I imagine it.

Duke jumps.

Lightning. Another one of his fears.

"It's here," Duke says, staring upward. His face is pale. "And it's bringing the pain."

"What?" I ask.

He clutches his head. "Me. It's about me. It's going to use my fears against everyone. It wanted me here. The beginning at the end."

"Justin?" It's Not-Mom.

I shudder and whip around. She stands at the edge of the backyard. She waves and smiles. Her teeth are black.

"Don't do this. If you stay, I'll get better. You can make me better. The Seeker can heal me, bring me back to you."

"Justin . . ." Lyric takes a step back, his eyes wide with sorrow. "Man, I . . ."

"Oh no . . ." Mary stares at the thick brush near the shed in the backyard. Red eyes appear. Then another pair. It's the rat snakes.

It's starting.

Mary takes a step toward the back gate as if she wants to make a run for it, but Duke grabs her.

"You can't leave. We have to play the game," he says.

Mary trembles. "But—"

"We've lost too much," Duke says. "I'm not going to let the Seeker steal one more minute of my life. We fight back. We go home." He makes eye contact with all of us. "That's all that matters. Leaving here. Destroying the monster once and for all."

Mary's moment of hesitation transforms into determination. She stands up straighter. "Okay, okay." She exhales a deep breath. "I'm ready."

Three creepy porcelain dolls step from around the house. They stand side by side in charred clothing. There are hollowed-out spaces where their eyes should be. Their faces are cracked and their heads are covered with ratty strands of yarn.

"Play with me. Play with me."

"They don't look so scary," says Carla.

Their sinister smiles widen with loud creaks and their bodies contort. Their heads spin around and they drop onto all fours, crawling toward us.

"Oh," says Carla.

Shae whimpers. We stumble back.

"Justin?" Not-Mom says. She ghosts closer as the rat snakes emerge from the thick brush.

I spin around and race toward the tree.

The ground shakes. Lightning streaks through the air. The bolt hits close to the tree, sparking a small fire. I stumble to a stop. Out the corner of my eye, I see Duke dive for cover.

Despite the heat of the flames, ice forms on the trunk of the tree and travels up and out to each branch. Icicles hang dangerously like frozen fingers.

A fuzzy blur emerges from within the tree. It is faceless, a human-shaped form about my height, with multiple red eyes. Black wings unfurl from its back. It extends its arms and sharp claws appear.

"Oh snap!" cries Lyric. "What is *that*?"

"What do we do?" Shae clutches Quincy's arm, tugging him back. "What do we do?"

This game *is* different. We're not playing against each other. We're playing against our fears and the Seeker. In its world, with its rules.

"I went up the hill, the hill was muddy, stomped my toe and made it bloody, should I wash it?" a deep, growly voice says.

Duke was right. The Seeker is here.

30

For a moment there's no response. We're all in shock.

"Everybody, go. Now!" I yell.

We scramble, hitting each other like out-of-control bumper cars as we scatter in different directions.

I duck down near the side of the porch. "Jus-tin," Not-Mom says in a creepy singsong voice. I flinch as her cold breath hits the side of my face. I squeeze my eyes closed.

Not-Mom's cold fingers slide down my arm.

"Go away," I whisper desperately. "Please go away!"

From my hiding spot, I peek toward home base. The monster is standing guard, not searching like it's supposed to do. It's using the fears to do its dirty work.

Mary screams. A giant rat snake has her by the ankle and pulls her across the backyard, away from her hiding spot.

Not-Mom grabs my arm in a bruising grip. I spin around and shove her away. She tumbles back, her eyes wide with shock. For a moment I'm frozen in horror. I pushed my mom. Her surprise morphs into fury. The hatred in her expression takes my breath away.

She springs forward. I slip out of her reach and race to help Mary before she is taken back to the well. I freeze, overwhelmed by the sight before me. Every fear has been unleashed. It's a war zone of terror. Attacks come from every direction.

The ground splits with a loud crack. Bowling ball–size bugs crawl out of the opening. They're beetle-like with sharp fangs. Horns protrude from their heads, and their scorpion-like tails sway back and forth.

Quincy stumbles back. He trips over his feet and falls on his butt. The insects quickly advance, then something flies past me and becomes embedded in the side of the house.

It's a needle. The kind nurses use to draw blood in hospitals. Another one zooms past me. I dive out of the way.

"Awwww, come on," Lyric cries as he bobs and weaves. "Nobody said anything about needles. Duke! Is this you?"

"Sorry!" Duke yells, dodging a needle.

"Man, how did you forget to mention this one?" Lyric asks.

"Wouldn't you forget this one if you could?"

Lyric spins around, then he freezes. He narrowly misses being hit by a needle.

"Get down!" I say.

His panicked eyes race around the backyard. He's breathing heavily. "Justin? Nia?"

Oh no! He can't see us.

"Lyric!" Nia calls out, but he doesn't hear her. He runs one way, backtracks, then goes in a different direction.

He's so disoriented, he's not concentrating on the fears approaching from every angle.

"They're still here. I just can't see them." His voice cracks. "It's okay. They won't leave me."

Shadowy figures slink across the ground toward him. They shift, peeling off the dirt, until they are standing. It's another one of Duke's fears. The shadows are in various human shapes—tall, short, wide, thin. They surround Lyric. He swings around, fists raised as they shoehorn him in and launch their attack.

"Justin," he cries. "Help me!"

I start toward him, but skid to a halt when Nia cries out. She hobbles around as if any movement hurts.

"Nia?"

She glances up at me, her shoulders hunched up to her ears.

Wrinkles appear on her face as tears stream down her sunken cheeks.

I glance down at my hands. The skin shrivels, too. My joints ache. Nia's pain is my pain. My heart pounds loudly in my ears. I can't . . . I grab my chest.

"You're weak. No one likes you. You have no friends." Carla faces off against a bigger, angrier, meaner version of herself. It stomps closer, with a smirk, until it's right in her face. It continues to shout as Carla withers from the insults.

"Shut up!" Carla yells.

Her double mocks her and laughs. "Shut up, shut up, shut up."

Can't breathe. I feel everything. It's too much. Don't know what to do, how to help. What's happening? What do I do?

"Somebody tell me where Justin and Nia are," Lyric says, his voice thick with tears. "Please! Where are they? Are they okay?" He takes a punch to the stomach and falls to his knees.

I struggle to answer, but the words won't come out. My throat is too tight. Everybody else is too caught up with their fears to answer.

"Keep them away! Keep them away!" Shae attempts to run for home base, but the creepy dolls block her path. One crawls forward and touches her arm, then her leg. Her skin turns white and hardens, becoming like porcelain. Shae tilts to the side and falls to the ground from the weight. Her limbs shatter. The doll side of her body is gone. She screams.

What— I stagger back.

The rat snake drags Mary closer to the backyard gate.

We can't win. We're not strong enough. I'm not strong enough.

I slap my hands over my ears to drown out the screams. Can't breathe.

"I can make it all stop," the monster says. I hear its voice inside my head. *"End the game. Declare me the winner and it will all go away."*

"Oh, baby," says Not-Mom. "Give in to us. We can take all your hurt and pain away. Stay here and we can be a family again."

I shake my head frantically, whimpering. She touches my face; it's gentle and warm. My eyes pop open. I gasp. It's my mom. Not my sick mom. My healthy mom. Her smooth brown skin is glowing. There is no smell of sickness or decay. She's wearing a bright red dress with large blue flowers. She's the most beautiful thing I've ever seen.

"Stay with me," she says. "Don't you want me back? We can be happy here."

I stare into her brown eyes, so much like mine. Her touch . . . It's been so long. I've missed this. I could forget everything else. I could—

A body slams into me and I hit the ground hard enough to rattle my bones. It's Nia. She scrambles away from me and curls into a ball, her arms circling her raised knees. "What's happening? Where am I?" Her voice is weak. Her hair has turned completely gray.

"Nia?" I reach for her. My hand shakes.

She flinches. "Don't touch me. I don't know you."

Her words tear through me. My memories shift, fading. I shake my head hard and make myself focus. Can't forget. Can't let her forget.

"Justin," my mom says.

I ignore her and take Nia's frail hand. "I'm Justin. I'm your best friend." She has to remember me, remember us.

Nia blinks, her eyes clearing before clouding with confusion again.

I swallow the mountainous lump in my throat. "Did you know you're the first person I called after my mom died? Did you know . . ." My voice cracks.

Her hand jerks in mine. I hold it tighter and stare into her eyes. *Come back to me, Nia.*

"Justin, let her go. I'm here now," my mom says, her voice loud and clear, tempting me to give in.

Nia, Nia, Nia. She's my friend. I need her. "Did you know I keep your emails and texts? When I feel down, I read them and I know I'll be okay. Please remember me."

Her head tilts, and she studies me closely. Her forehead creases. She squeezes her eyes closed. Tears slide down her face. The war continues to rage around us, but I wait.

Her expression clears and her eyelids lift. My entire body shakes. She *sees* me.

"Did you know people go through 396 friendships in a lifetime, but only 33 will last?" She smiles. It trembles, but it's there. "You will be one of my 33."

I exhale a breath that shakes my entire body. She throws her arms around me and holds on tight. "I remember you, Justin."

We separate and stare at each other. She flinches as the volume of the screams increase. My gaze travels around and lands on Lyric. He's struggling to fight off the shadows.

"Let's go get our friend. Let's win this game and go home." I pull her to her feet. We both wobble before standing strong.

"No," Mom yells.

I peek over my shoulder. She looks crushed. I've disappointed her.

The Seeker cackles. I swing around to see it staring at something near the side of Zee's house. It's a girl. Her image flickers in and out. She's wearing a knee-length yellow dress and a flowery headband holds back her short locs.

She flinches and glances down at her wrist. She opens her mouth to scream, but there's no sound.

"Number four hundred," the Seeker says with glee.

Oh no! It has another kid. It looks like she's not completely here yet, but she's tagged. She's on her way.

"Nia, you have to hurry and get safe!" I say. "We have to make sure the Seeker doesn't cross over."

"But—"

"You have to touch home base," I say.

She stares at me for a moment, then glances at the tree. "What about you?"

"I have to help the others."

"But—"

"Go!"

She nods and hobbles toward the tree. Her movements are slow, unsteady.

Mary and the rat snake are directly in her path. I snatch up the pepper spray.

"Keep going," I shout at Nia when she hesitates.

Holding tight to the canister, I spray the mist into the rat snake's face. My eyes water as the breeze blows some of the chemical back in my direction. With a bloodcurdling screech the rat snake rears back and tosses me to the ground, but it releases Mary. Crying, she rolls away.

"Safe!" Nia hits the tree. Almost immediately, her aging reverses. At the same moment, the girl in the yellow dress, number four hundred, fades away. With Nia now safe, she's reduced the count. The Seeker roars and its blurry form vibrates with fury.

"Mary, get up. Get to home base."

She scrambles unsteadily to her feet and limps toward the tree, dodging the needles that continue to fly in our direction.

Another rat snake paws at my leg. Its claws pierce my jeans. I cry out as I feel the warm trickle of blood down to my ankle. Duke rushes toward me and jumps in the air. His feet slam into the rodent-reptile that has me pinned to the ground. The force of the impact sends the rat snake sailing across the backyard.

"Safe!" Mary calls out as she touches the tree. The rat snakes disappear. The Seeker lets out a screech that sends chills racing through my body.

"Tell Lyric I'm safe and that Justin is coming to help him," Nia says to Mary.

Mary relays the message.

Lyric shudders with relief. "Hurry up, Justin. I need you, man." He spins out of reach of one shadow and kicks another in the chest, sending it flying backward.

"We have to keep working together," Duke says, panting. "That's the only way to win."

I nod. "We take them out, one by one."

I start forward to help Lyric, but Not-Mom is back before me. Her skin peels off her face. "You're not leaving me!"

I stumble back, keeping my eyes on her. "Duke, help Lyric!"

Not-Mom continues to rant in my face. She takes my arms and shakes me. "You're not leaving me."

Duke dashes forward and suddenly a wall of spiderwebs appears. He swings his arms to get past them, but they cling to his body like sticky ropes. "Can't. Get. Them. Off," he pants out as they begin to wrap around him, cocooning him.

"Use the Swiss Army tool," Nia yells.

It's lying on the ground a few feet away from him. He struggles to reach it, but his feet and legs are completely locked together by the spiderwebs.

"Help!" Quincy screams. "It hurts!"

"Get away from my brother!" Carla shoves past her double and stomps toward Quincy, who is on the ground completely covered by the insects. She's holding a can of Silly String from the backpack. She fires it at the beetle bugs. The spray goes all over their bodies, making it harder for them to move. They hiss and scurry around, falling onto their backs. Carla stomps the bugs while they lie there. The crunch turns my stomach.

"Run, Quincy," she says.

Quincy crawls to his feet, then staggers toward home base. He launches himself at the tree. "Safe!"

The ground shakes beneath our feet. Trees topple over and wisps of eerie fog slink across the ground, evaporating. "*You'll pay for this,*" the Seeker growls.

Carla tries to run, but her double blocks her path.

"Nobody will come to help you. They don't like you," the Carla double says. "They don't want you to go home. They'll save everybody but you. They think you're a weak, mean bully."

Carla stumbles back. "Shut up! Leave me alone!"

Shae cries out. The dolls have surrounded her. She's more doll than human now. Her face is porcelain and even her hair is yarn-like.

Lyric continues to battle the shadows. They are brawling all over the yard.

Duke grunts and falls to his knees. He's now cocooned up to his chest. His arms are pinned to his sides. Black and brown spiders, the size of golf balls, appear and crawl all over his chest and face. He shakes his head violently, trying to get them off, but they cling to him.

I have to help. "Let me go!" I struggle against Not-Mom's grip, but she tightens her hold.

The Seeker cackles. *"So much fun. I love to play. More. More."*

The Carla double shoves Carla, forcing her back a few steps. "Everybody knows the real you. You're selfish. They only like your brother. One day he won't like you either. You'll have no one."

"Stop! Stop!" Carla says, covering her ears. "I give up. Make it stop."

I freeze.

Carla spins around to face the Seeker.

"I want to make a deal," she says.

31

The monster slinks forward.

"Don't do it," Lyric cries, as he's held down by a shadow.

The other fears stop, like we're taking a terror time-out.

Carla walks closer to the tree, toward the Seeker. She wipes tears off her face. "If I give up, quit playing, will you let me go home? Leave me and my brother alone for good?"

My heart races. This can't be happening.

"No, Carla," Quincy pleads. "Don't."

"You'll trap us here," Mary yells.

Not-Mom holds me close. I shudder. I hear her raspy breathing, feel the sickness seeping from her skin.

"You want to end this?" the Seeker asks. Its voice is deep and sinister.

Dark clouds swirl angrily above us and lightning flashes, the bolts streaking repeatedly like fireworks, like they're celebrating a victory.

If she doesn't finish the game, we've broken the rules. The Seeker wins again. Our punishment will be even worse than the first time.

"Carla, if you betray us, it will take over our world, too. It's lying to you. You'll never be safe." I try to take a step forward, but Not-Mom holds me back. Her bony fingers tighten like handcuffs.

"You can be with me forever, baby. Isn't that what you want?" she whispers in my ear. I shudder.

"Repeat after me," the Seeker says to Carla. *"No more running and hiding, no more games to face. By taking this deal, I'll forever leave this place. I've picked a side and this is the end. I choose the Seeker and not my friends,"* the monster chants.

Even though it's faceless and I don't see an expression, I feel its glee. Is this what it made Hyde and Zee say? Is this how they were released?

"Carla, please—" Duke says, his voice muffled. The webs partially cover his mouth.

"You can't leave us here," Shae says. Tears fall from her marble-like eyes. The dolls surround her.

Carla flinches, but creeps closer to the Seeker.

The others are huddled around the tree yelling and begging Carla not to betray us.

"Guess I am selfish," she says, then turns to the monster. "No more running and hiding, no more games to face."

A cry rips out of me. I fall forward onto my knees.

"By taking this deal, I'll forever leave this place," Carla says.

It can't end like this. It can't. My lungs seize. I'm gasping for air.

Carla takes another step forward, and her foot catches the strap of the slingshot lying near my backpack. She stops before the Seeker. Its excitement is billowing off its form in waves.

"I've picked a side and this is the end," Carla says. "I choose myself, and save my friends." She lunges forward and touches the tree. "Safe."

Poof! Her double disappears.

My heart jumps, stops, then jumps again.

"What just happened?" Lyric asks with wild eyes.

Carla snorts. "Like I was gonna let some stupid monster beat me. I may be selfish, but I'm not weak and I can be smarter than all y'all when it really counts."

My jaw drops. She didn't betray us. She played the Seeker.

"I knew my sister would save us," Quincy says. "Yay, Carla."

"Now finish it so we can go home." Not removing her hand from the tree, Carla kicks the slingshot. It sails through the air and lands next to Lyric.

For a moment no one moves. Then everything happens at once. The monster roars. The sound is so hate filled that I feel it in my bones. Its fury is alive, and on a mission to seek and destroy.

Lyric dives away from the shadows, grabs the slingshot and a few rocks off the ground. He fires them at the dolls near Shae. One rock hits a doll in the chest. A crack forms. The body sways and hits the ground, shattering. He fires again and another doll goes down, then he's pulled back by a shadow creature.

"Grab the rope," Quincy shouts. He holds one end and the other end is near Shae. She takes hold of it and, with one hand still on the tree, Quincy drags her closer. Mary and Nia use their free hands to help as well.

Shae hits the trunk with a whimpering, "Safe." The remaining doll vanishes. Shae's limbs reappear and all her doll features fade.

Lightning bolts zigzag down, striking the ground around us. Patches of grass catch fire. A trail of flames shoots toward Duke.

I break free from Not-Mom and run toward the Swiss Army tool on the ground near Duke. I knock the spiders away and use the blade to slice through the webs cocooning him. Gasping for air, he falls forward against me. We dive out of the path of the flames, but they follow our movement. The heat is painful.

"Let's go!" I pull him toward Lyric. "We have to help him."

Now the odds are even. Duke and I square off against two shadows, leaving Lyric to battle the other one.

We're wrestling across the backyard, trying to avoid the lightning strikes and stalking flames.

"Lyric, get safe," Duke yells.

"Where's Justin?"

"He's with me," Duke says. "We've got this. Go!"

Lyric hesitates, then runs toward the tree. He smacks it. "Safe!"

Nia gives him a one-armed hug. They're safe. A weight eases off my chest.

"Justin," Not-Mom yells. "You can't leave. I won't let you." She appears next to me and takes my face in her bony hands. "You're mine."

Duke starts toward me.

"No. Get safe! That'll take out all your fears."

"We finish it together," says Duke.

"This is on me." Yeah, they can see her, but Not-Mom is my fear.

Duke stares at me, still unsure. With haunted eyes, he nods. He understands. Some battles you have to conquer alone. He dashes toward the tree, leaping over flames, dodging needles and lightning bolts.

The others are urging him on, waving frantically.

"Hurry!"

"You can do it!"

"Run!"

He lifts his hand to touch the trunk, then stops. His palm is inches from the bark.

"What's wrong?" Mary asks. "What are you waiting for?"

Slowly, he turns to face the Seeker. The monster creeps closer.

"Having doubts? This is your home," it says.

Duke stares at it, his expression cold and disgusted. He takes in every inch of the monster's form, slowly.

"Hyde and Zee . . . they were a means to an end. But you . . ." The Seeker's black wings flap, as if it is waving Duke forward for an embrace. *"You're mine. There were other kids I could have taken first, but you were special. Strong. The perfect child to begin my world."*

Duke's face crumbles. Tears slide from the corners of his eyes. "Why?"

The Seeker's head tilts. *"Why not? Someone always has to start the game. There's always a player number one."*

Duke jolts. His tears dry up as he gawks at the Seeker.

"There's nothing for you back there now, but here you have me."

"Eighty. Years," Duke says, shaking with fury. "Hiding, running, playing your twisted game. I might have been your beginning. But now I get to be a part of your end." A cold smile tilts his lips. He slams his palm against the tree. "Safe!"

In an instant, the needles fall to the ground. The shadows and flames disappear. The lightning sizzles out. The webs float away on a cool breeze. The spiders vanish. Duke is free and fearless.

The monster trembles violently, then tosses back its head and howls. The others may have weakened it by making it to home base, but Duke *wounded* it. Cheers erupt, muffling the Seeker's rage.

I yank my arms out of Not-Mom's grip. Now it's my turn. The Seeker zooms forward and stands next to her scary, decaying corpse.

"It's over," I say, my voice shaky.

Not-Mom leans down so our faces are almost touching. I fight not to gag as I smell her rotting flesh.

"I love you."

Tears fill my eyes and trickle down my sunken cheeks. "My mom did, but you're not my mom. She's . . . she's . . . dead." The words cut my throat.

"I can be alive if you want me to," Not-Mom says.

I blink and her appearance changes again. Her long hair grows until it reaches her shoulders. Her eyes are bright and smiling. She smells like sunshine and honeysuckles.

"Stay with me," she says. "Don't you want me back? We can be happy here."

"This isn't real. You'll change back like before," I whisper.

In the background, I hear my friends calling to me. I turn in their direction, but she forces my head back around and cups my face. "It can be real if you want it to be," she says. "Stay. We'll be happy together. You won't feel so lost anymore. This is where you belong, with me."

I place my hands over hers on my cheeks. She smiles and my heart grows warmer in my chest. Good memories of my mom play like a movie in my head. I'm happy.

"I'm your safe place," she says. "Remember this?" She extends her arm and opens her closed fist. A puzzle piece rests in her palm.

I gasp and reach into my pocket. My piece is gone. How—

"This is from our last puzzle together. You didn't finish it because that would mean I was gone forever, right?"

I swallow hard and nod.

"We can finish it together. Look." She points across the backyard. Only it doesn't look like the backyard anymore; it's my house. The kitchen. A puzzle sits on the table. "Once this one is done, we can start another one. We don't ever have to finish. We never have to end."

She takes my hand in hers and leads me away from the tree and my friends. Their voices fade away. In a daze, I follow. My body doesn't feel like my own. Her soft, calming voice is in my head, telling me how smart, funny, and strong I am. She makes plans to cook all my favorite meals, to take me to all the places we never got to travel to.

Her hand tightens around mine. I glance down to where she holds me and spot the 399 on my wrist. The mark. The Seeker. I stop abruptly and my head jerks back up to my mom. She smiles encouragingly. I blink and a shadow passes over her face. The decaying corpse reappears. Not-Mom.

"You're not real. I want you to be, but you're not." I yank out of her hold. "My real mom wouldn't want me living with my fear forever. She'd want me free."

The Seeker's growl makes my knees wobble.

"Justin!" my friends yell.

I spin around to see them waving for me to hurry. I race toward the tree.

Not-Mom ghosts around me to block my path. "You don't love me. If you did, you wouldn't leave."

I dodge her and run faster, fighting the heavy wind that pushes me back. Almost there. My friends are jumping up and down, waving me forward. Their support gives me an extra boost of energy.

"*You'll regret this,*" a deep voice says.

With a running leap, I hit the tree. "Safe."

Nia and Lyric pull me into a strong embrace.

The vultures hiss, lifting off from the roof. They dive low and attack Not-Mom. Their claws scratch at her face and arms as she waves them wildly over her head to protect herself.

"They eat the dead," Nia whispers. I turn away, unable to watch.

Nowhere is crumbling, turning on itself.

The Seeker's form grows taller and wider until it's a giant pulsating blob. "*You think it's over now?*" the creepy voice says. "*That you've won?*"

Duke glances at me. He starts to fade away. I catch my breath. What's going to happen to him when he gets home? I realize I don't know his last name, or where he's from. I don't know if he has brothers or sisters or anything about his family. I never asked and I'm sorry. He helped save us. He risked everything knowing what this would mean for him. I may not really know Duke, but I know he is my friend and I know what I need to say.

"Thank you."

His eyes are bright. He glances around at the fading world around us, then turns back to me. "It's finally over. Thank *you*."

I blink and he's gone.

"What's happening?" Shae asks.

"We're going home," says Nia, her voice awed.

I hear a loud gasp. Mary holds up her hands and slowly vanishes.

"You'll never be free," the Seeker says, his angry voice echoing in my ears.

"You've lost," says Lyric.

"This is just one game. There are many more."

"What does that mean?" asks Nia.

The monster cackles. *"You think I'm the only one?"*

Shae disappears.

"This feels weird." Carla vanishes.

"I have friends, too. And my *friends have their own worlds, their own games with rules,"* the Seeker says. *"Where I failed, they'll succeed."*

"Whoa," says Quincy, then he's gone.

"You'll regret this day."

Nia squeezes my hand and fades away.

"If you come for us again, we'll be ready," Lyric says as he disappears.

Only I remain.

"I am the Seeker. You can't hide. I will find you. You'll never be safe," it says.

My head spins. More than one monster? I'm wearing a giant bull's-eye. But all that matters is today I'm free. Today we've won.

I glance across the backyard. The birds fall to the ground with a horrifying shriek. Not-Mom is nothing but a pile of bones. The puzzle piece flutters to the ground beside her. The unfinished puzzle sits on the table.

The world around me fades in and out, flickering as if it's short-circuiting. It could be my imagination, but in the distance, I think I hear kids cheering. They're free. This place can no longer hold them. The heaviness that has weighed me down from the first moment I arrived disappears. My arm stings. I glance down and see the 399 change back into the swirly pattern on my skin. I'm no longer numbered.

"I'll see you soon, Justin." The Seeker's form expands, then explodes.

I'm blinded by a bright light. I'm weightless, floating, and then there's nothing.

32

I jolt awake, breathing heavily. My entire body is sore and my head pounds. I blink and look around. I'm lying on the floor in . . . in . . . I jerk up. I'm in my mom's room. My fingers dig into the faded carpet. We did it. We made it home!

Wobbling, I climb to my feet and burst out of the room. "Victoria!" The house is silent. My gaze swings around, taking in everything at once. It's the most wonderful place in the world. As I race to the front door, my eyes fall on the picture of my mom. I stop and walk toward it on shaky legs. For a moment, I'm hit with the memories of Not-Mom, but then something shifts in my chest. Love defeats the fear. All I feel is happiness. Happiness that I had my mom for eleven years. I have to treasure every moment, good and bad, and I know it's time to let go, too.

"Justin!"

That's Lyric. I fling open the front door and step outside into the blinding sunlight. Lyric and Nia race down the street toward me. Behind them are Shae, Carla, and Quincy.

We're safe!

Zee is, too. We understand what he went through in Nowhere now. We can help him get better, help him come back to us.

I reach for the puzzle piece, then I remember it's gone. That's okay, though, because I have my friends and sister. They're living, breathing pieces that fit together to form something cool and special.

My family.

33

Butch barks loudly and scratches at the front door. Hyde opens it and steps outside onto the porch. The dog races inside, whimpering. "What—"

A melody catches Hyde's attention. Whistling. He glances down his driveway. A girl strolls toward the house. Her head bops left and right to the beat.

"This is private property," Hyde yells as he steps forward, now standing at the top of the stairs. The girl continues forward, her long brown hair brushing against her shoulders.

"I said . . ." He falls silent as the girl stops close to the porch.

"Not happy to see me?" she asks.

"Do I know you?"

"You don't recognize me?" She pouts. "I guess it has been a long time. Nine years."

"Nine . . ." He sucks in a loud breath. "Mary?"

"Hi, Brother," she says with a wicked smile. "I've been waiting for this day a long time. We have a lot of catching up to do."

Hyde stumbles back. "I . . . What are—"

"You like games, right?" She marches up the porch steps. "Let's play."

ACKNOWLEDGMENTS

Thank you to my family and friends for the prayers, support, and encouragement. Please know I appreciate you all.

Thank you to my awesome agent, Emily Keyes from Fuse Literary, who believed in this story and decided to take the journey with me.

To my amazing and brilliant editors, Matt Ringler and Shelly Romero, and the super Scholastic staff: copy editors, designers, sales, marketing, publicity, and every other person who helped get *Hide and Seeker* out into the world. It is because of all of you that this book is better than I ever could have imagined.

Shout-out to my sisters (Shae, Kiesha, and Sonya), my cousins

(Gabriel, Antawan, Tiffani, and Kevin), and all the kids in the neighborhood. You were willing and sometimes unwilling players in hundreds of games of Hide and Seek. Thank you for the scares, the memories, and being the inspiration for this story.

Thank you to my nephews, Sean and Cameron. You are Justin. You are heroes.

Dad, you are my biggest cheerleader and never let me forget it. I'm so happy I get to share this moment with you.

Mom and Grandma, look what we did! I miss you both every minute of every day. All that I write, all that I am, is because of you. I feel your love. I hear your laughter. I see your smiles.

To Amy, Mary Alexa, Merisa, Deirdre, Camela, Michelle, Amaani, and Consuelo, who saw the struggle over the years, sent treats, made me laugh, kept it real, and never let me give up.

Thank you to Emily L., who read the first draft of *Hide and Seeker* and gave me feedback on sticky notes. Friend, I will always be grateful for your never-ending support.

To my writer friends and critique partners (Toni, Amanda, Mikko, Renee, and Aimee), thank you for the late-night talks, texts, and emails. You read the manuscript again and again, guided me through each and every revision, cheered me on when I was discouraged, and celebrated with me when my dream came true. I will never be able to thank you enough.

Above all, I want to thank God for His blessings and favor. Without God, none of this would have been possible.

ABOUT THE AUTHOR

DAKA HERMON was born in Tennessee and spent her childhood huddled under a blanket with a flashlight, reading and writing fairy-tale and fantasy stories. She works in the entertainment industry and is an active member of the Society of Children's Book Writers and Illustrators. She loves peach sweet tea, chocolate, cupcakes, and collecting superhero toys. Daka lives in California and can be found online at dakahermon.com and on Twitter at @dakadh.